THE ODD APOTHECARY

APPRENTICE EDITION

Created by

Donovan Scherer

The Odd Apothecary: Apprentice Edition

FIND YOUR POTION AND MORE AT
The Odd Apothecary

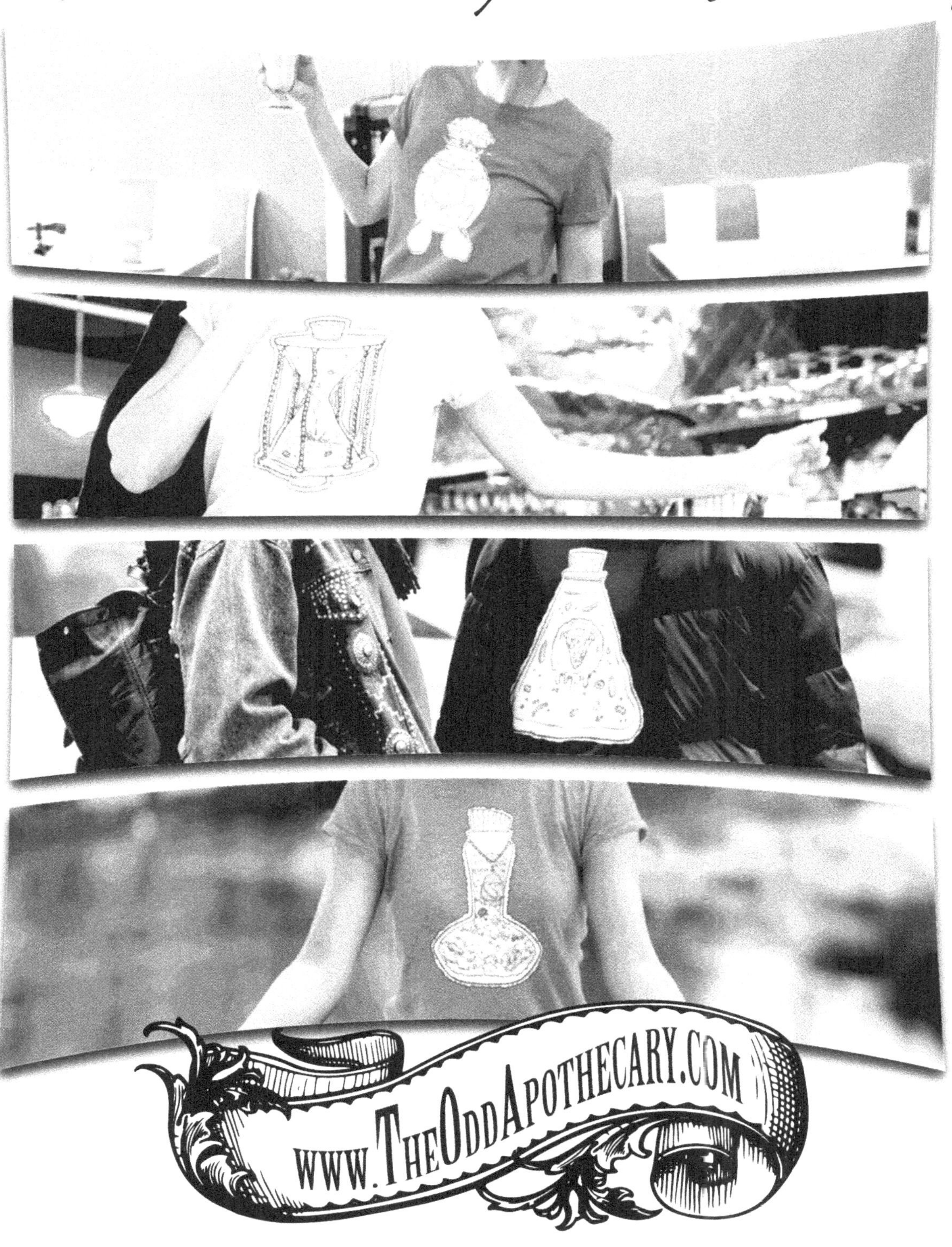

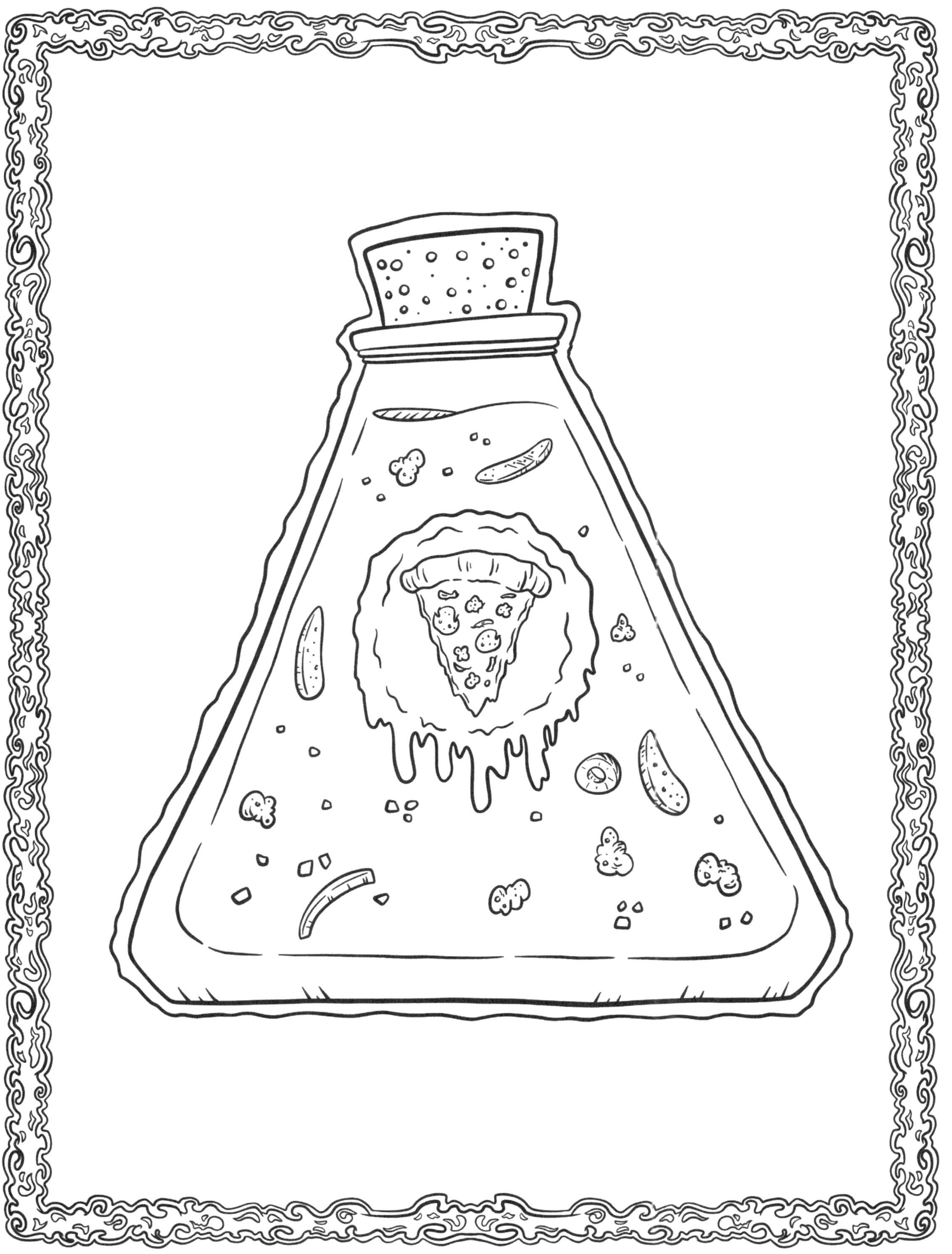

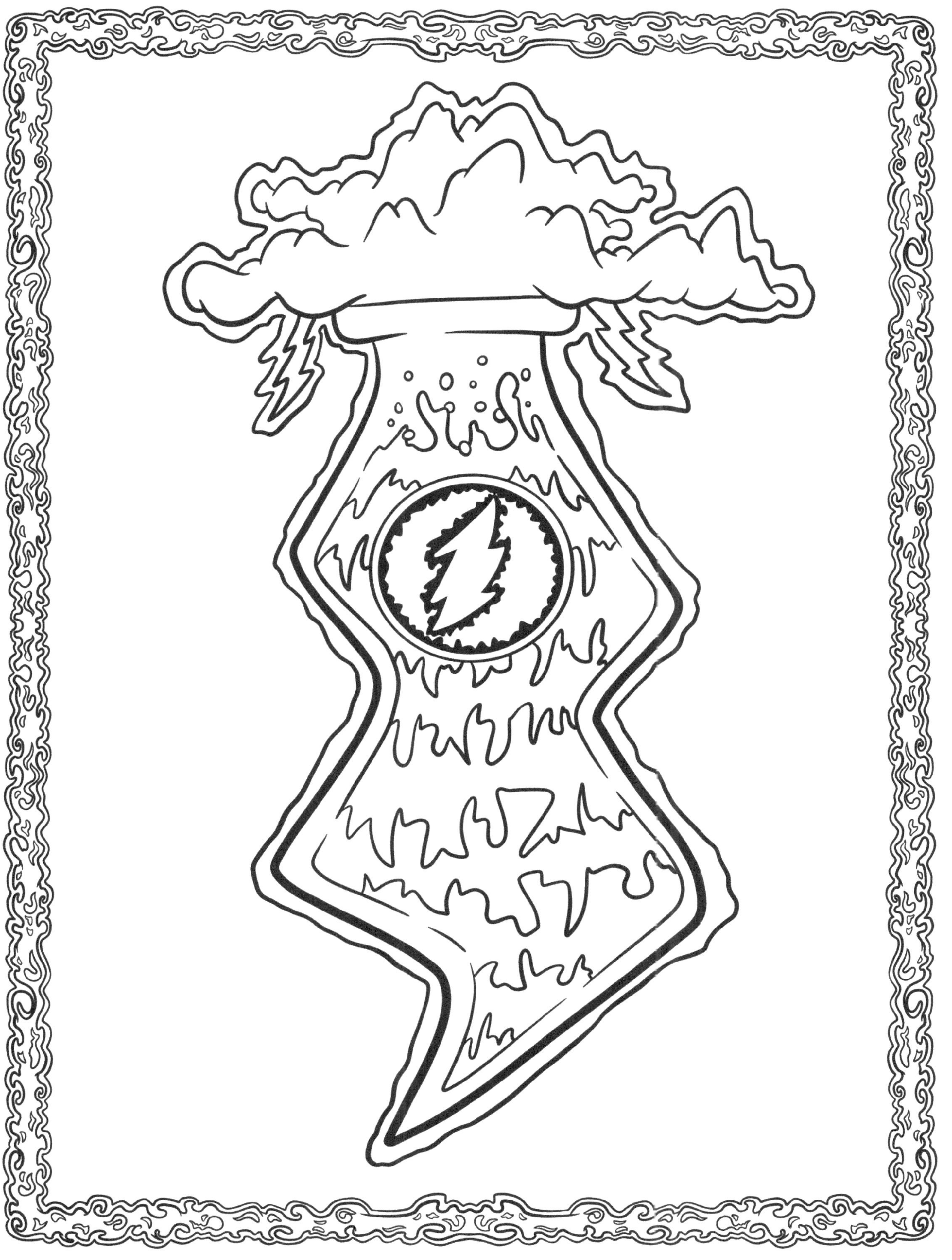

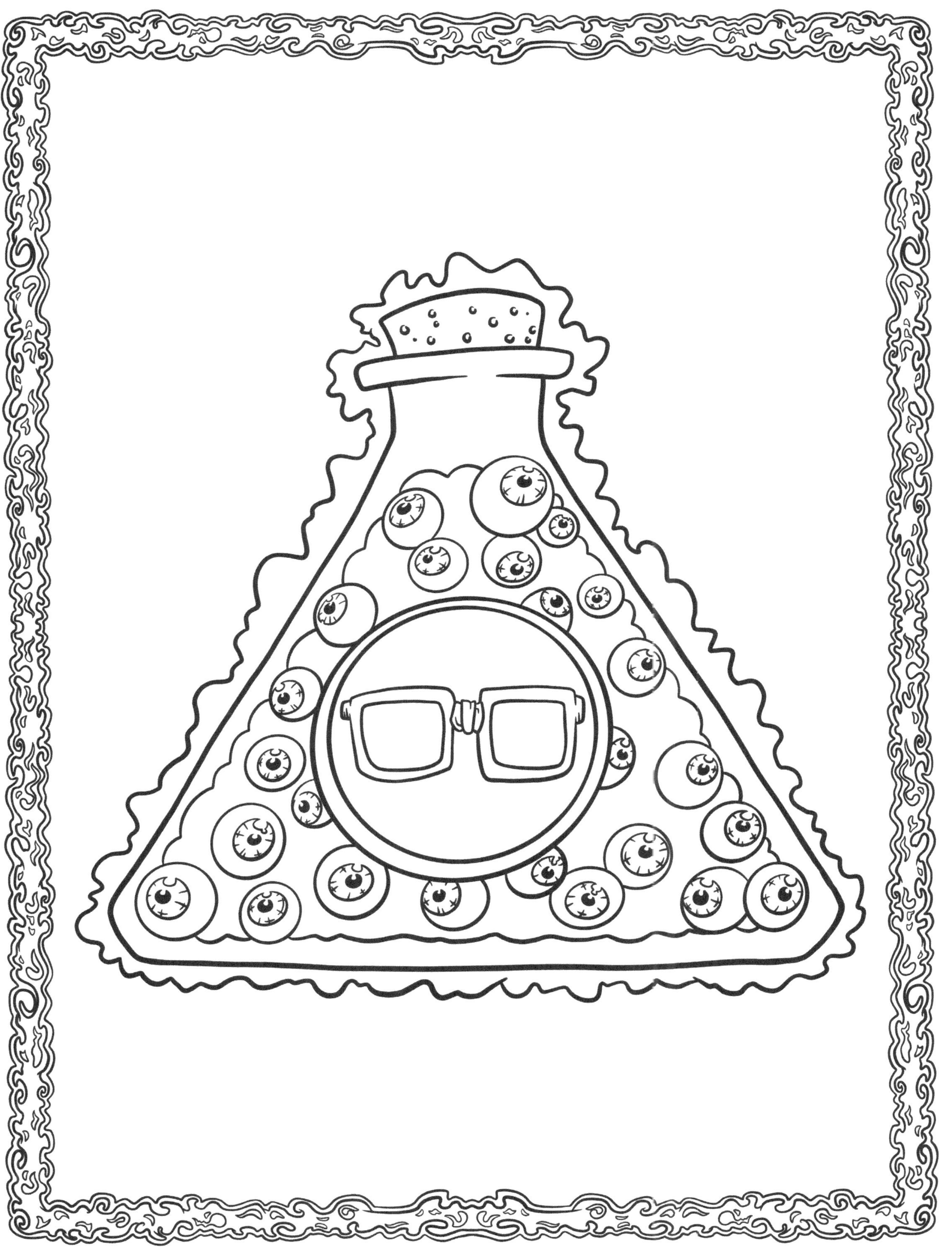

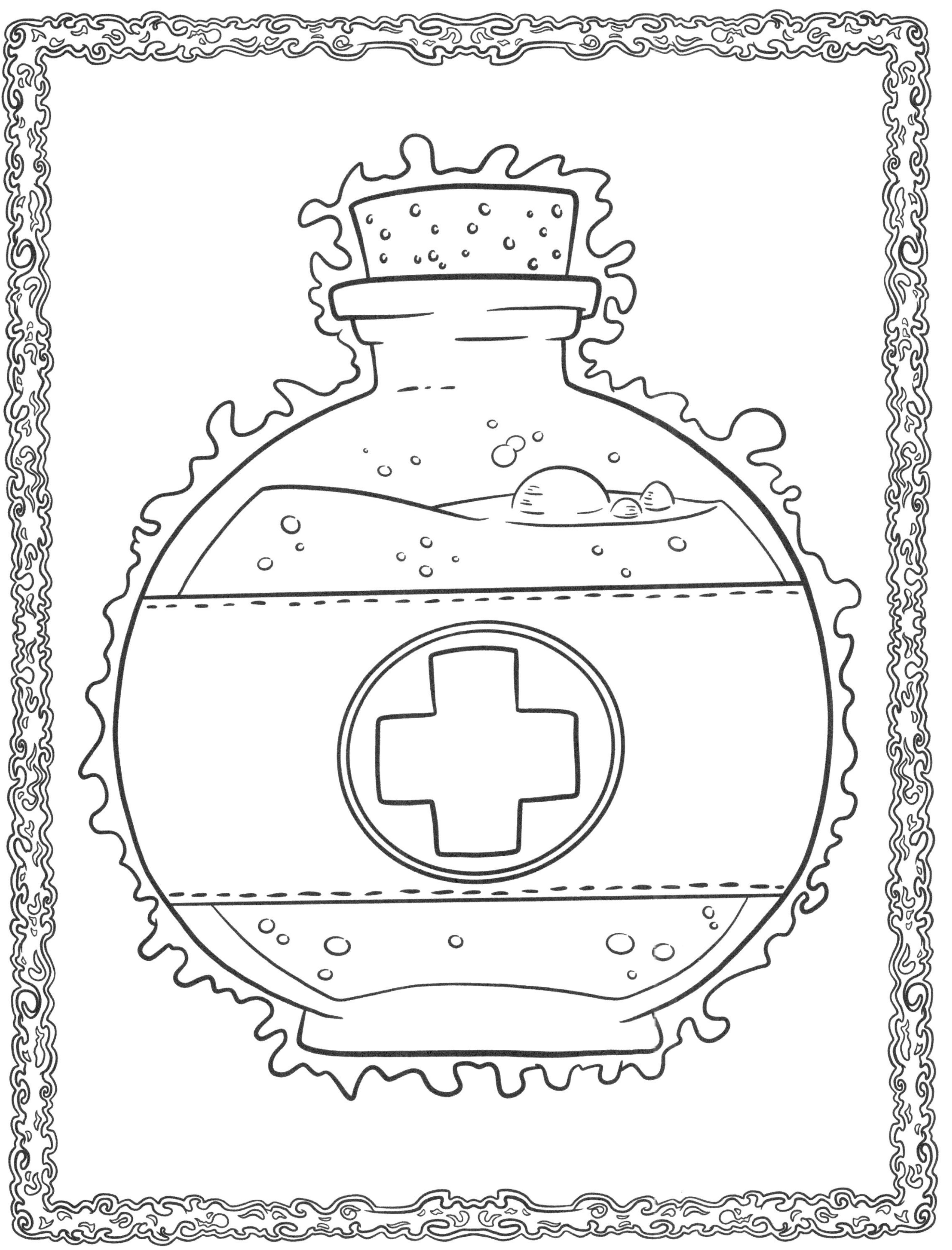

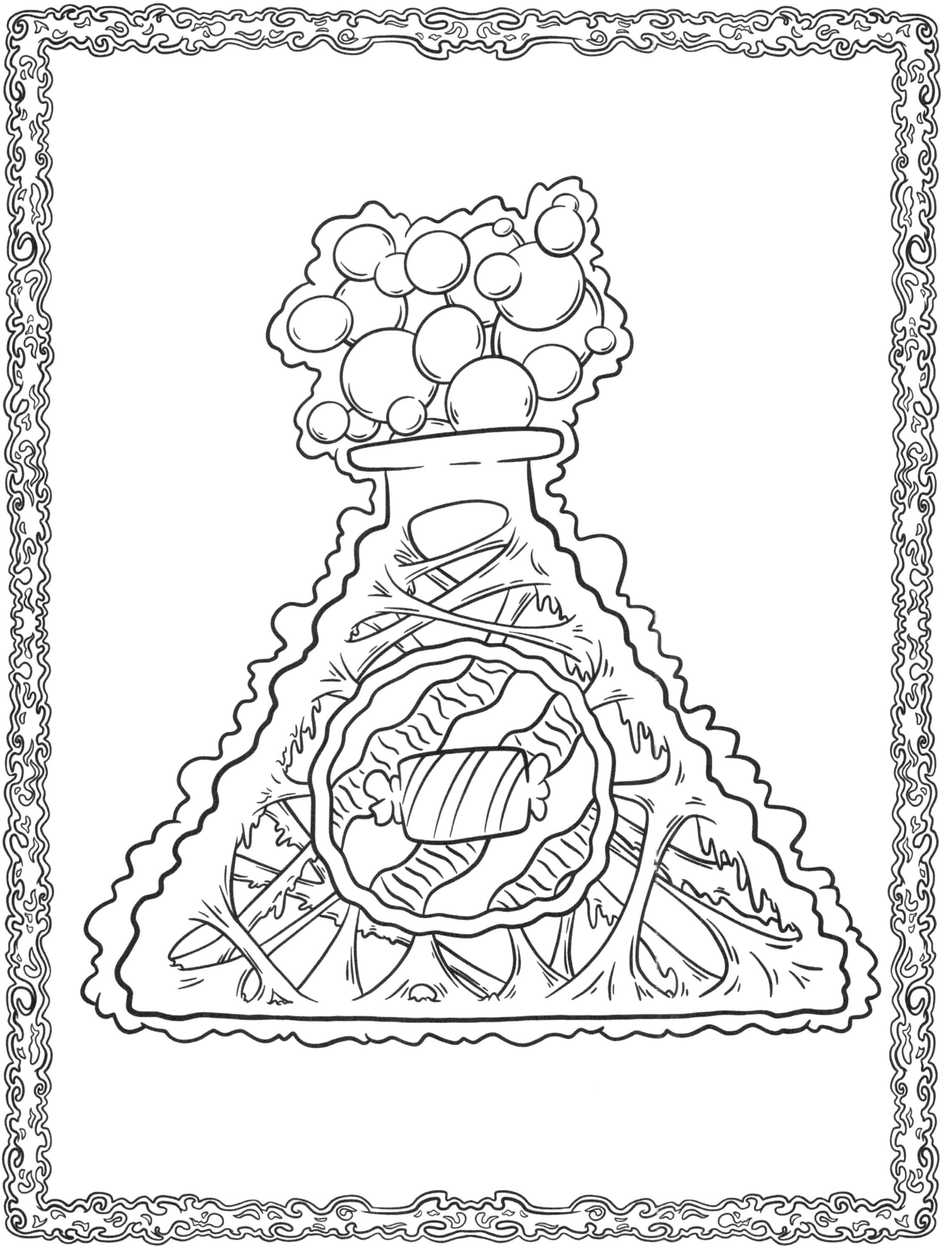

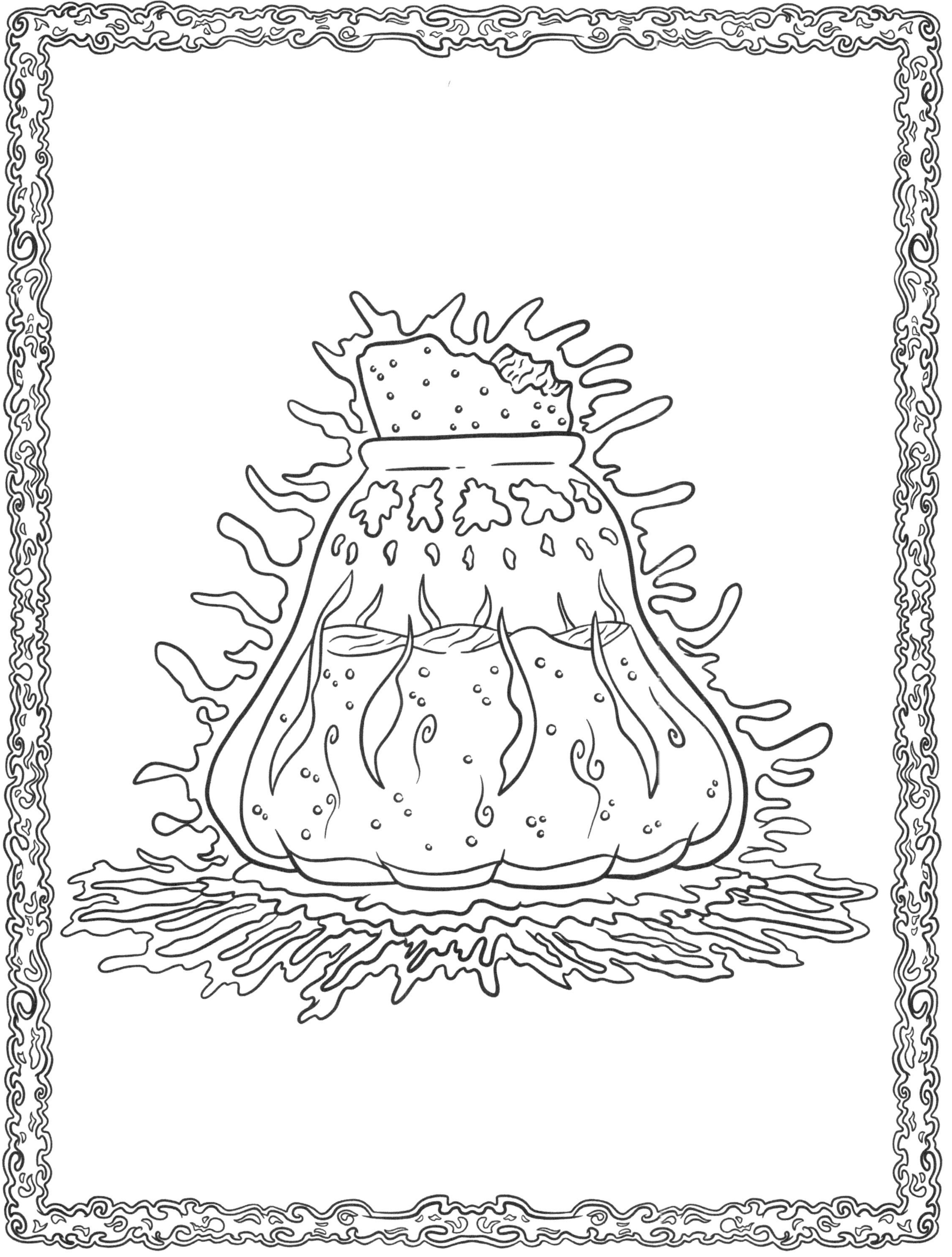

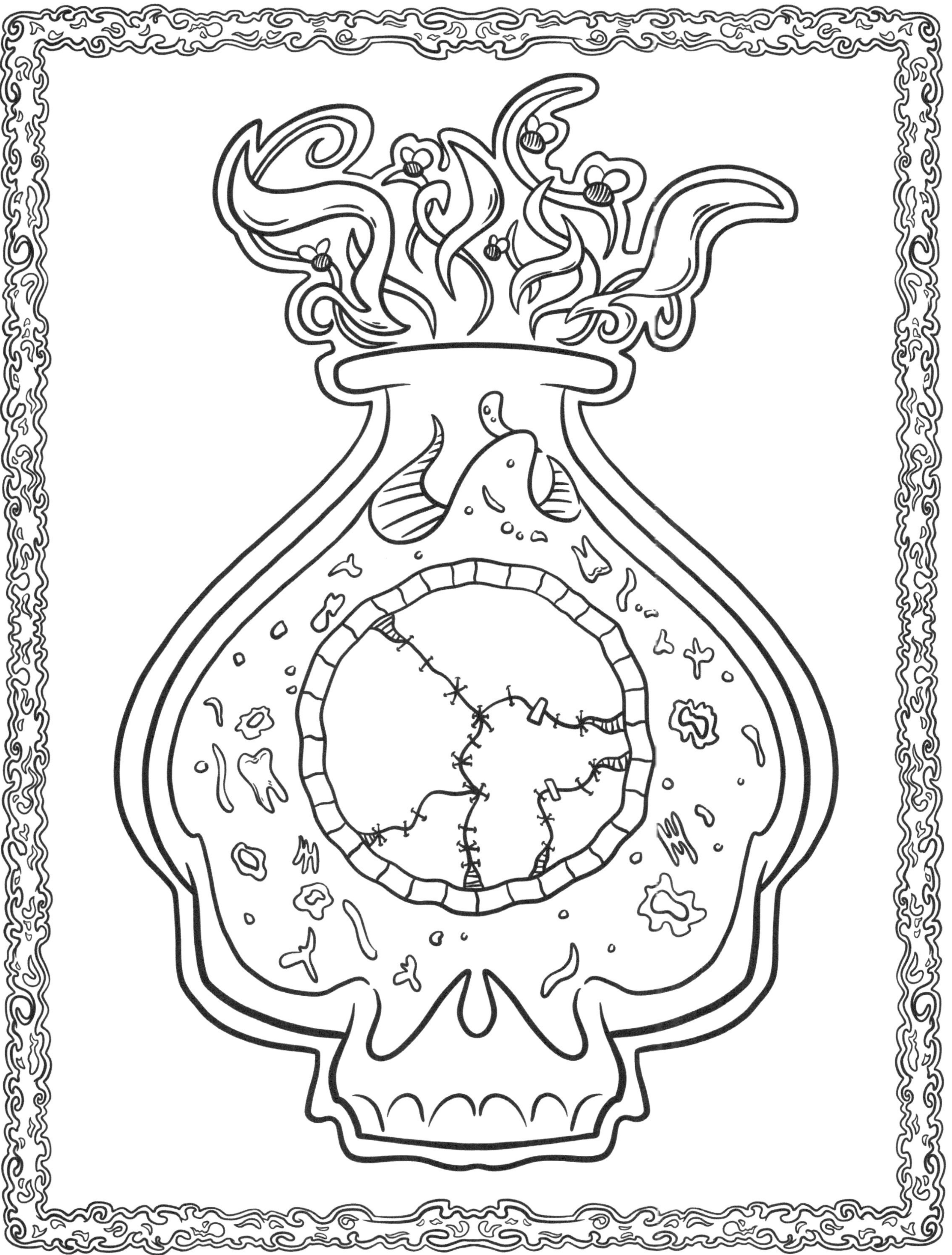

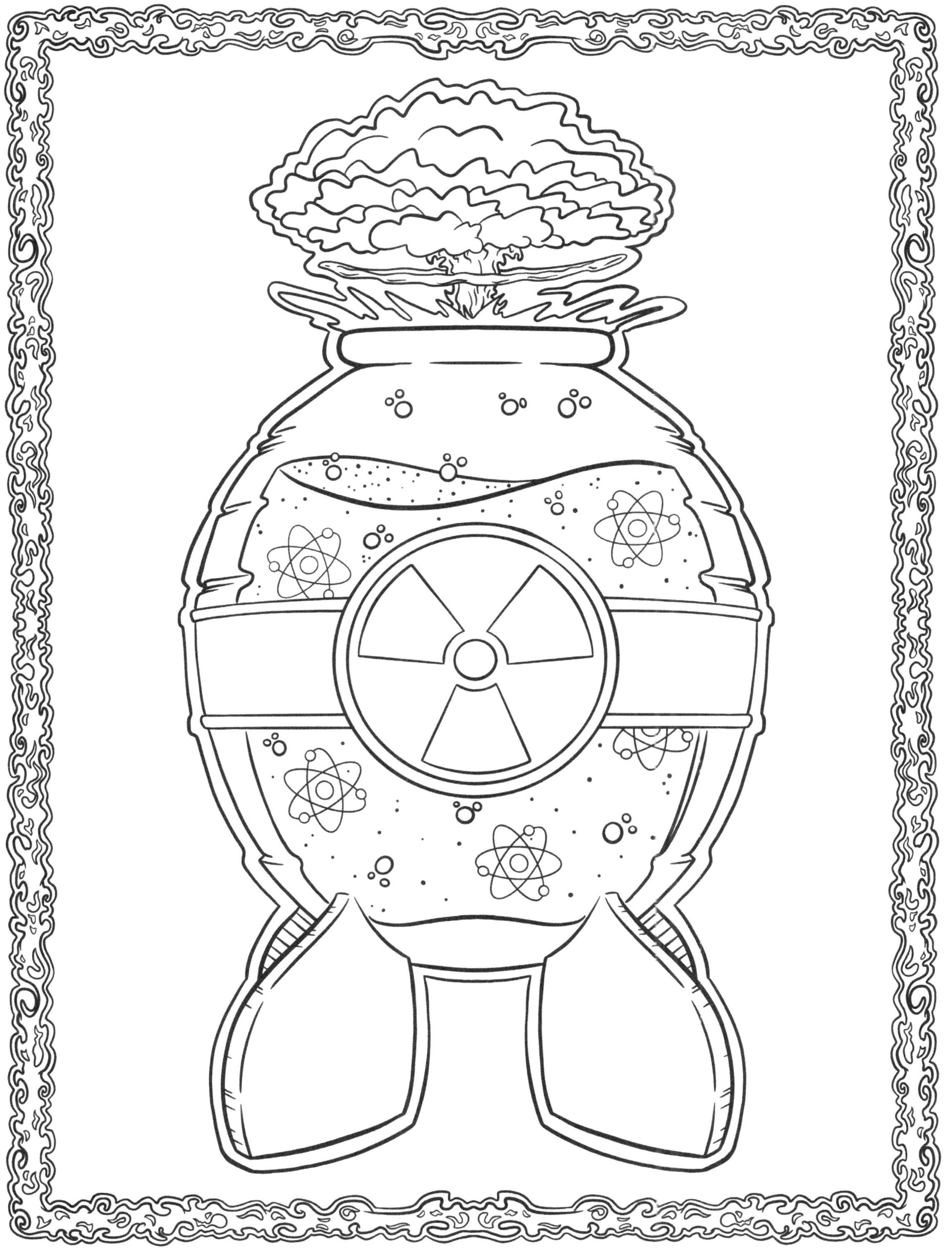

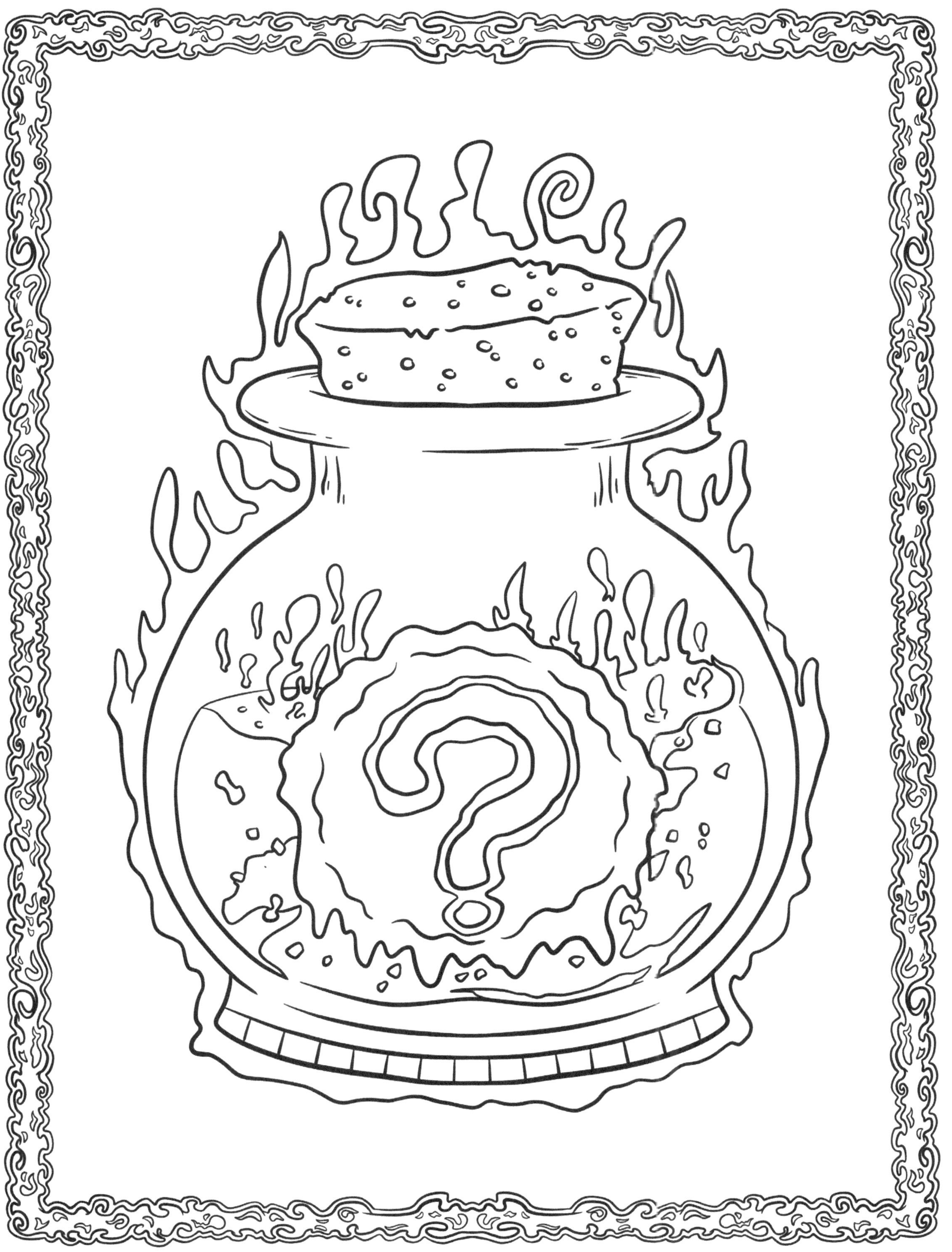

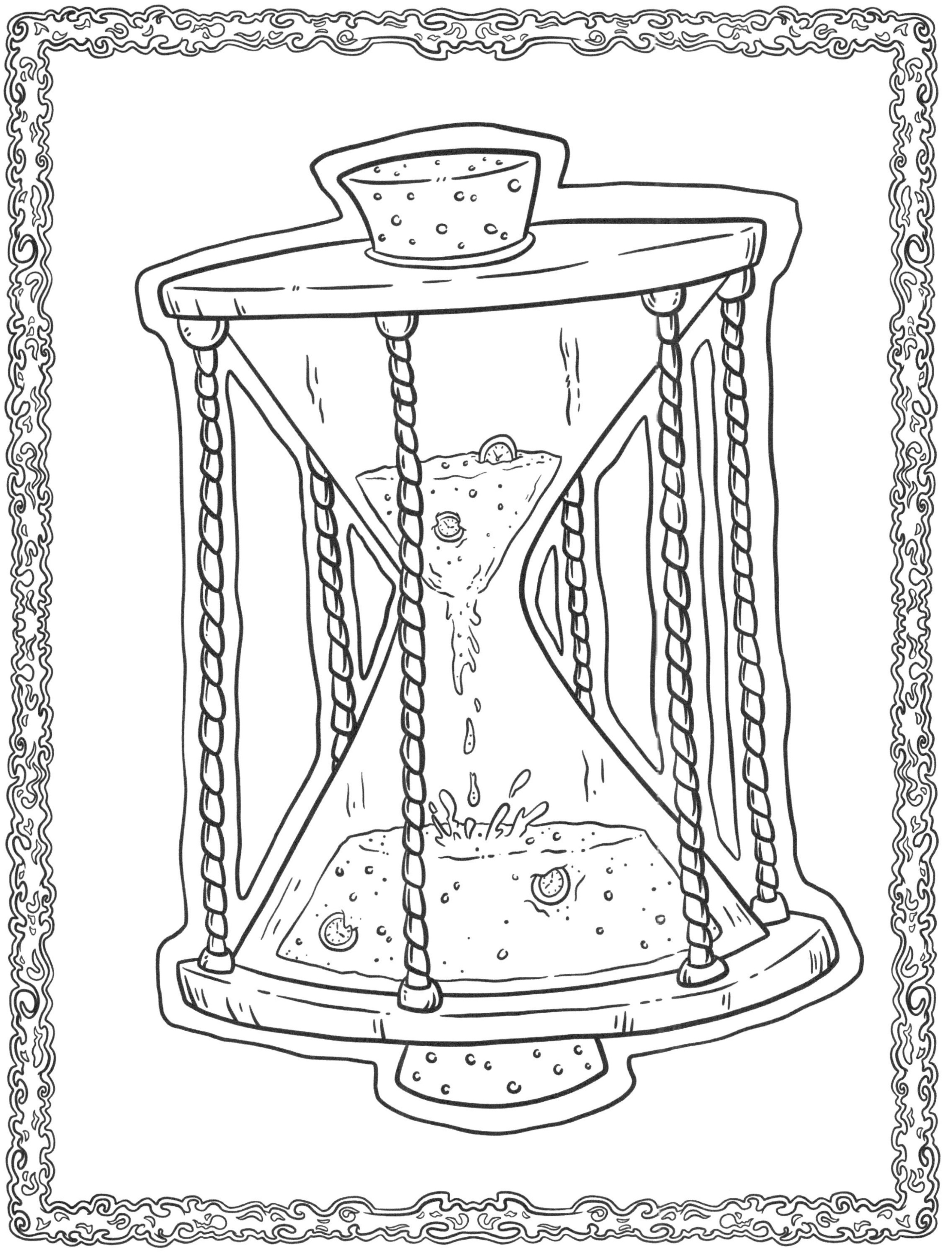

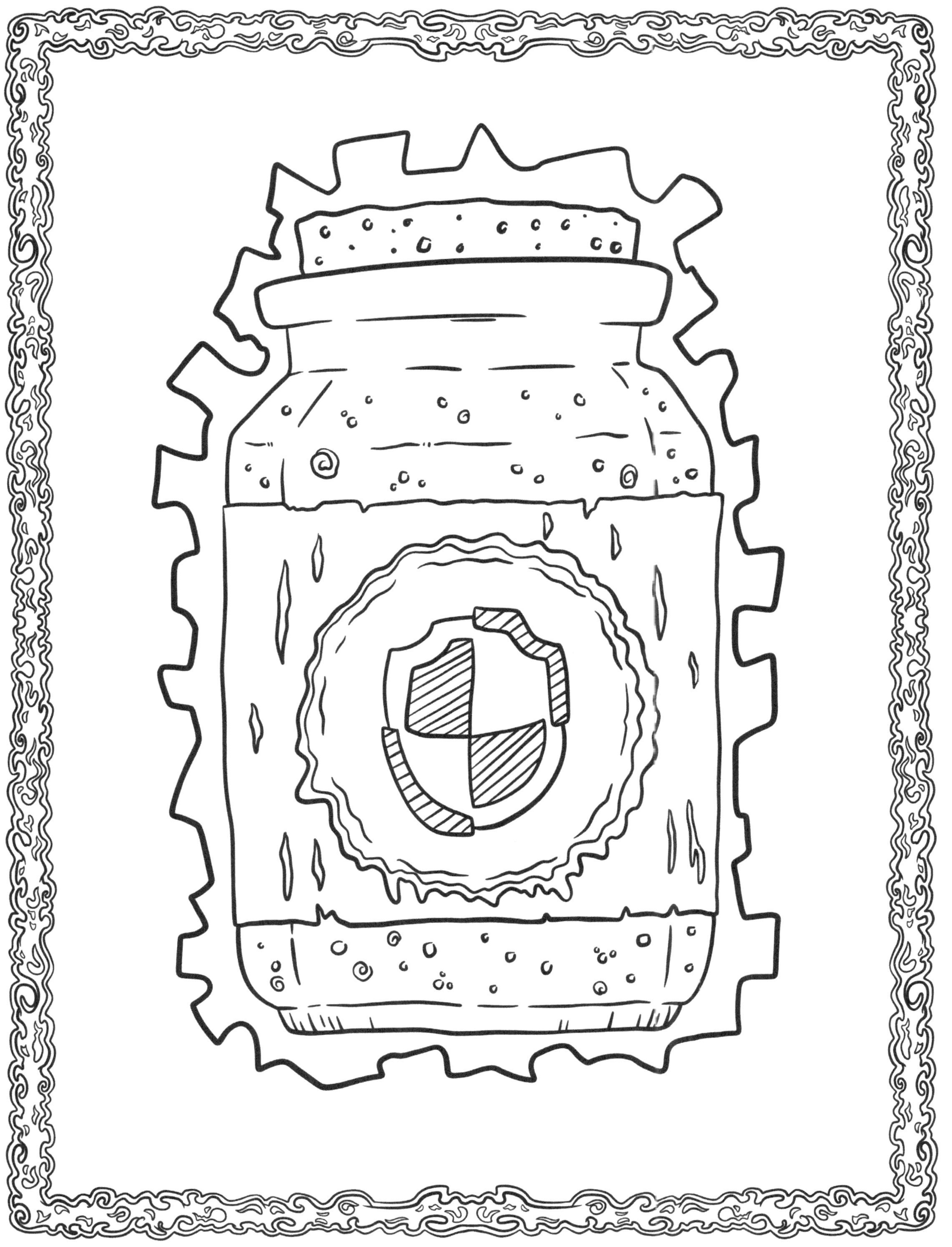

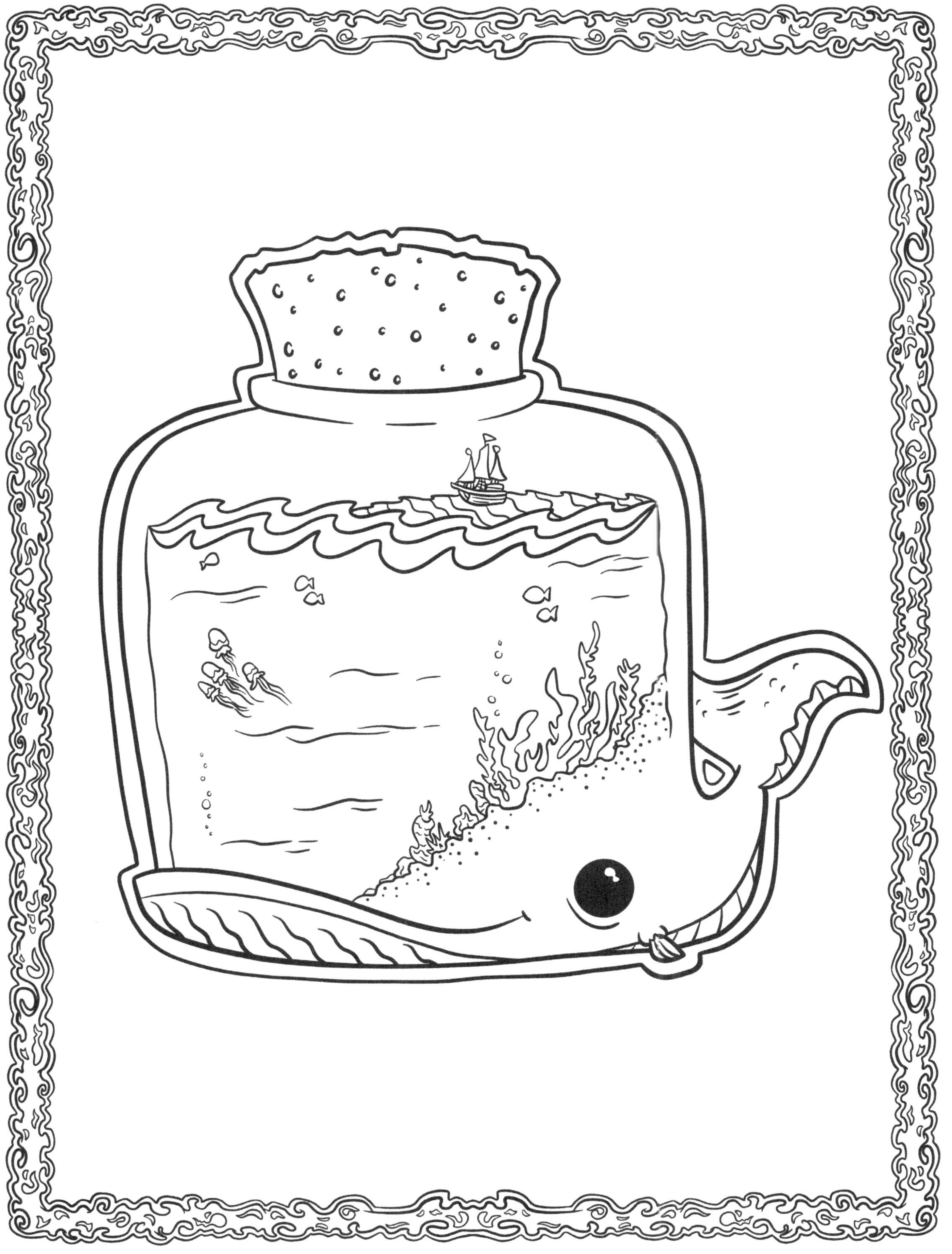

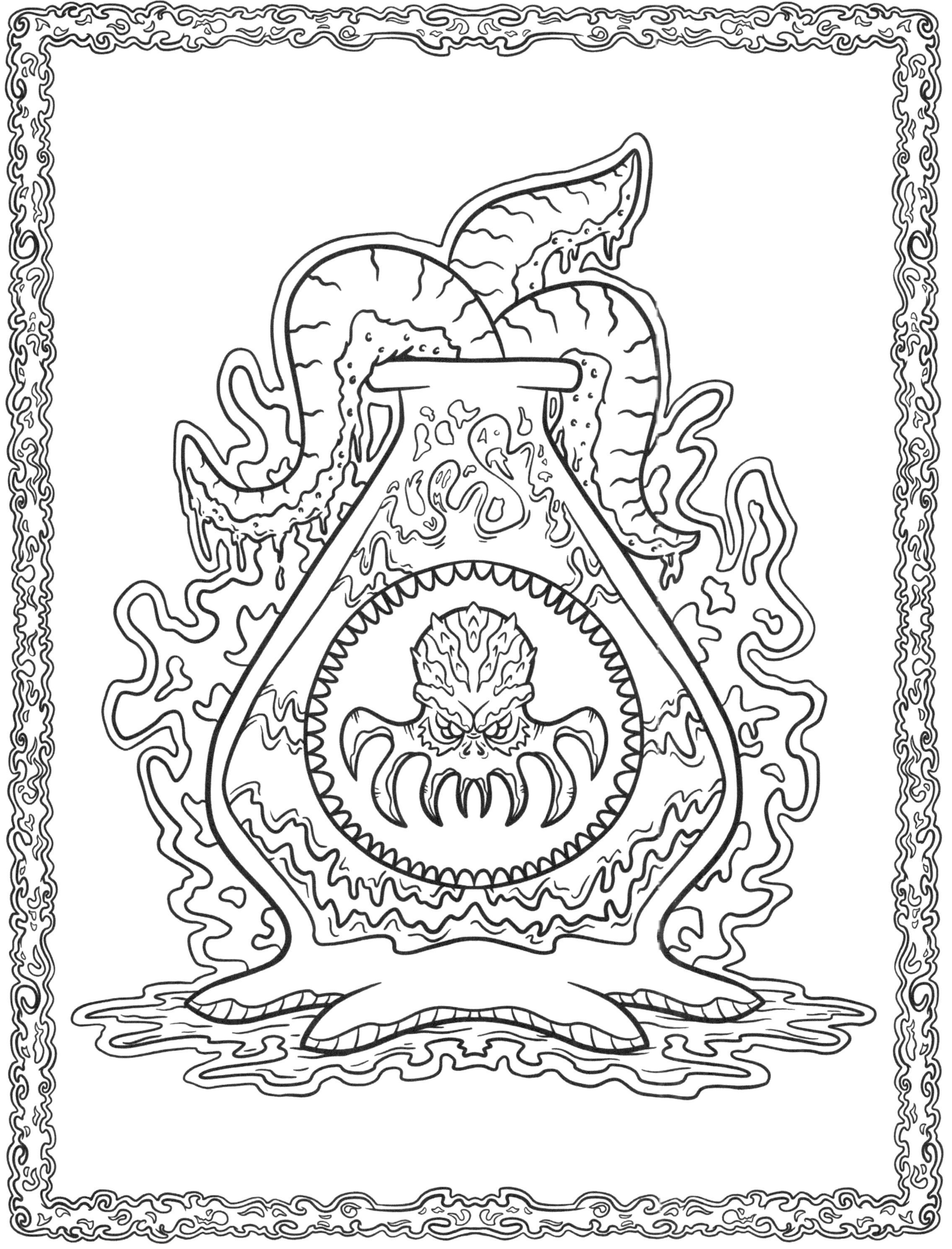

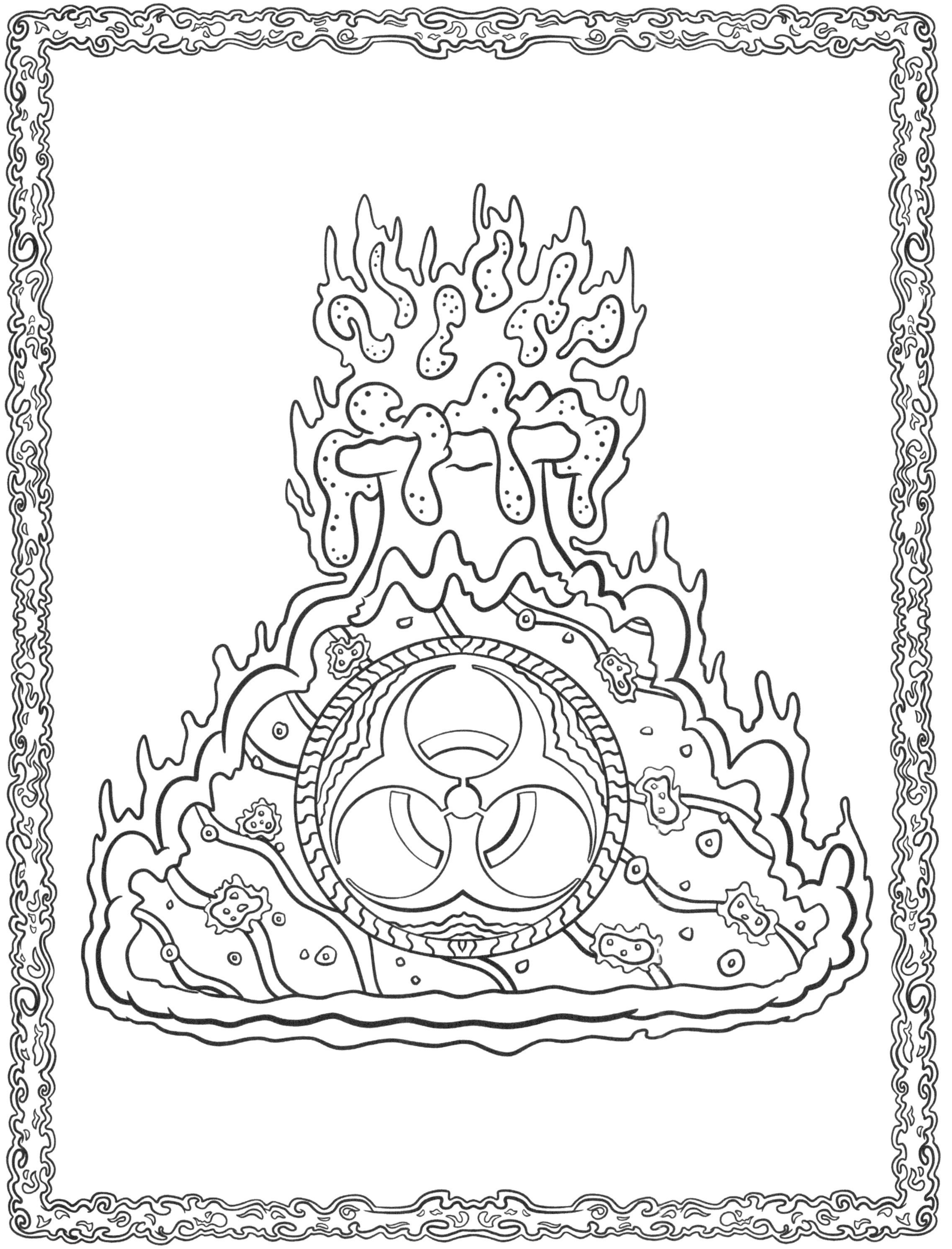

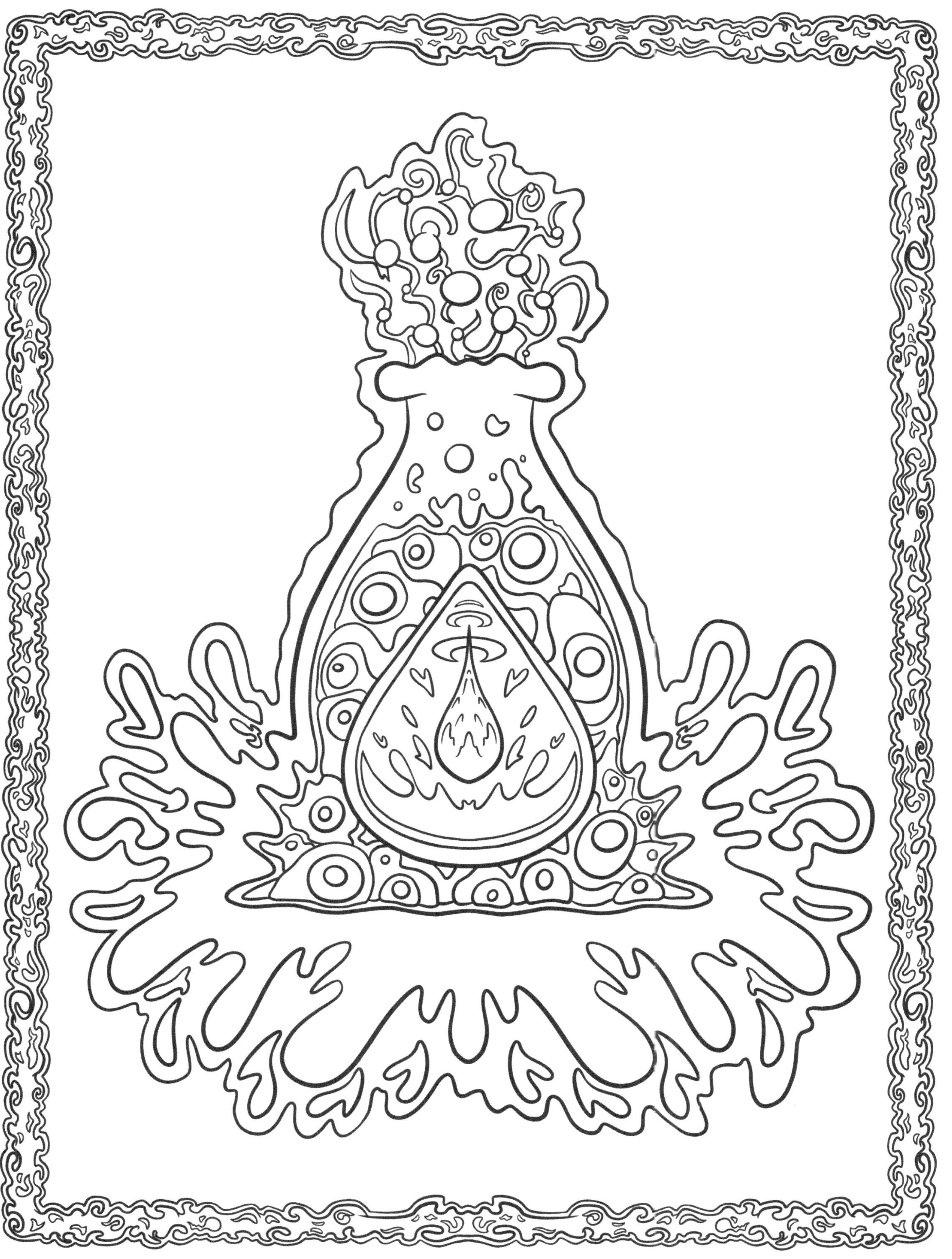

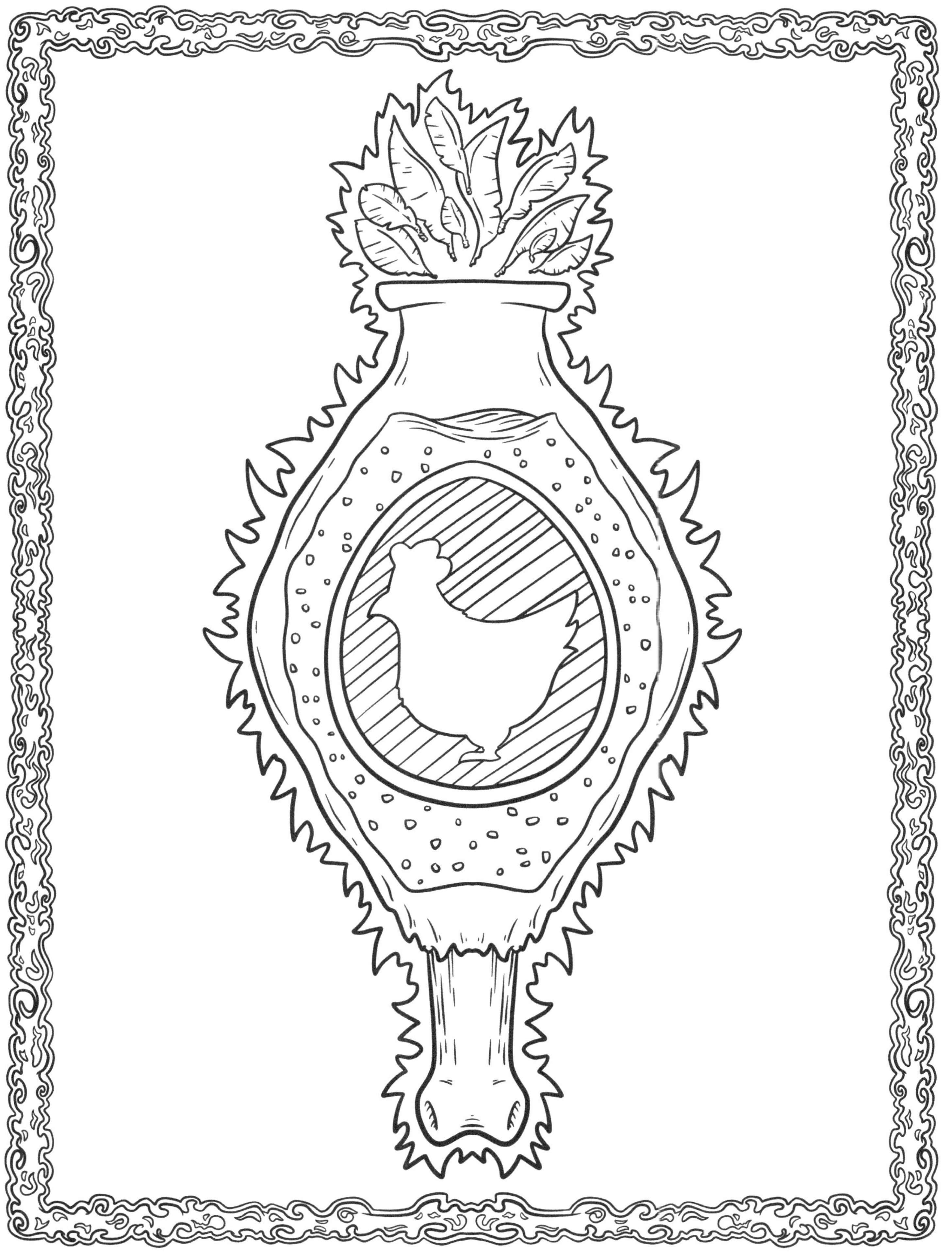

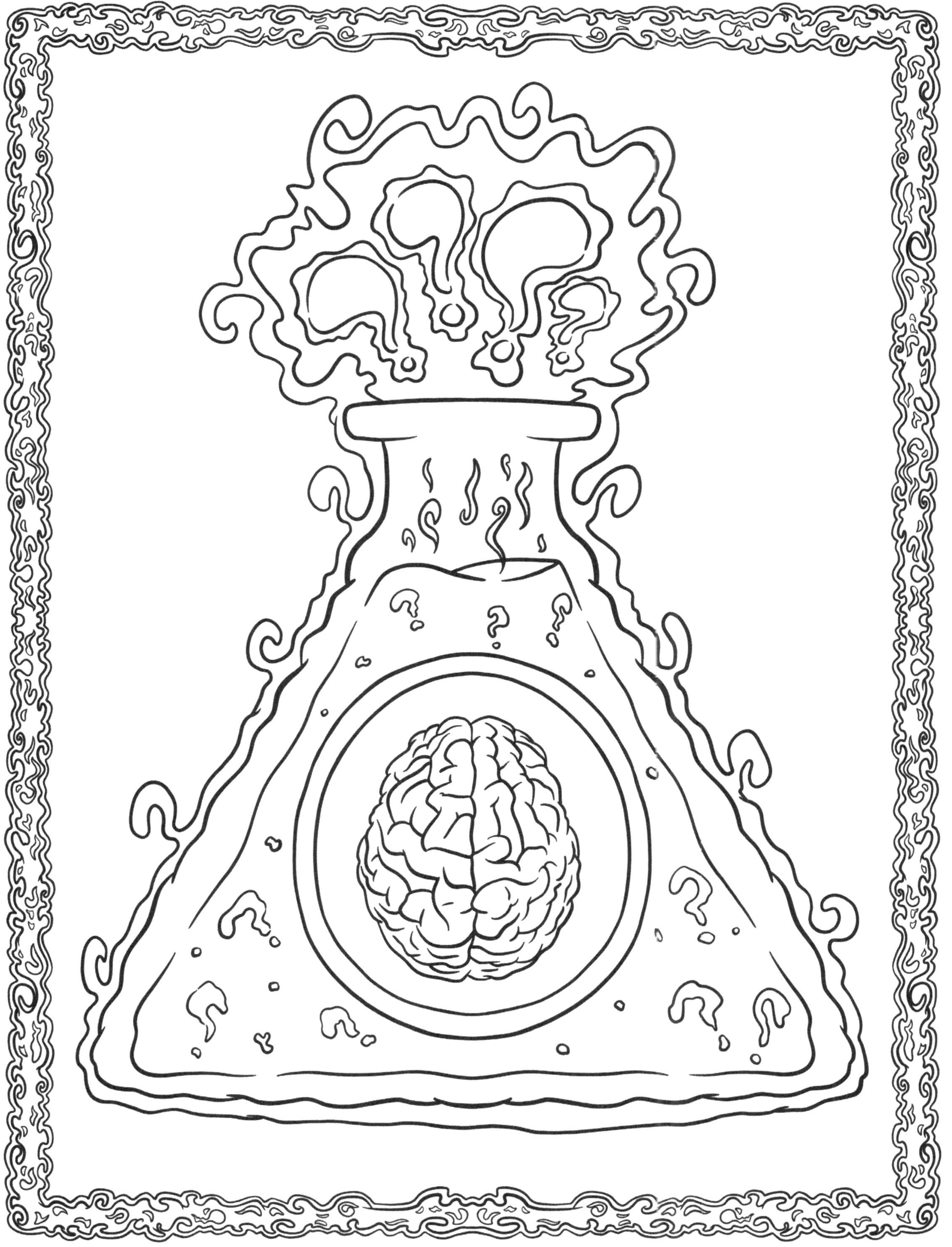

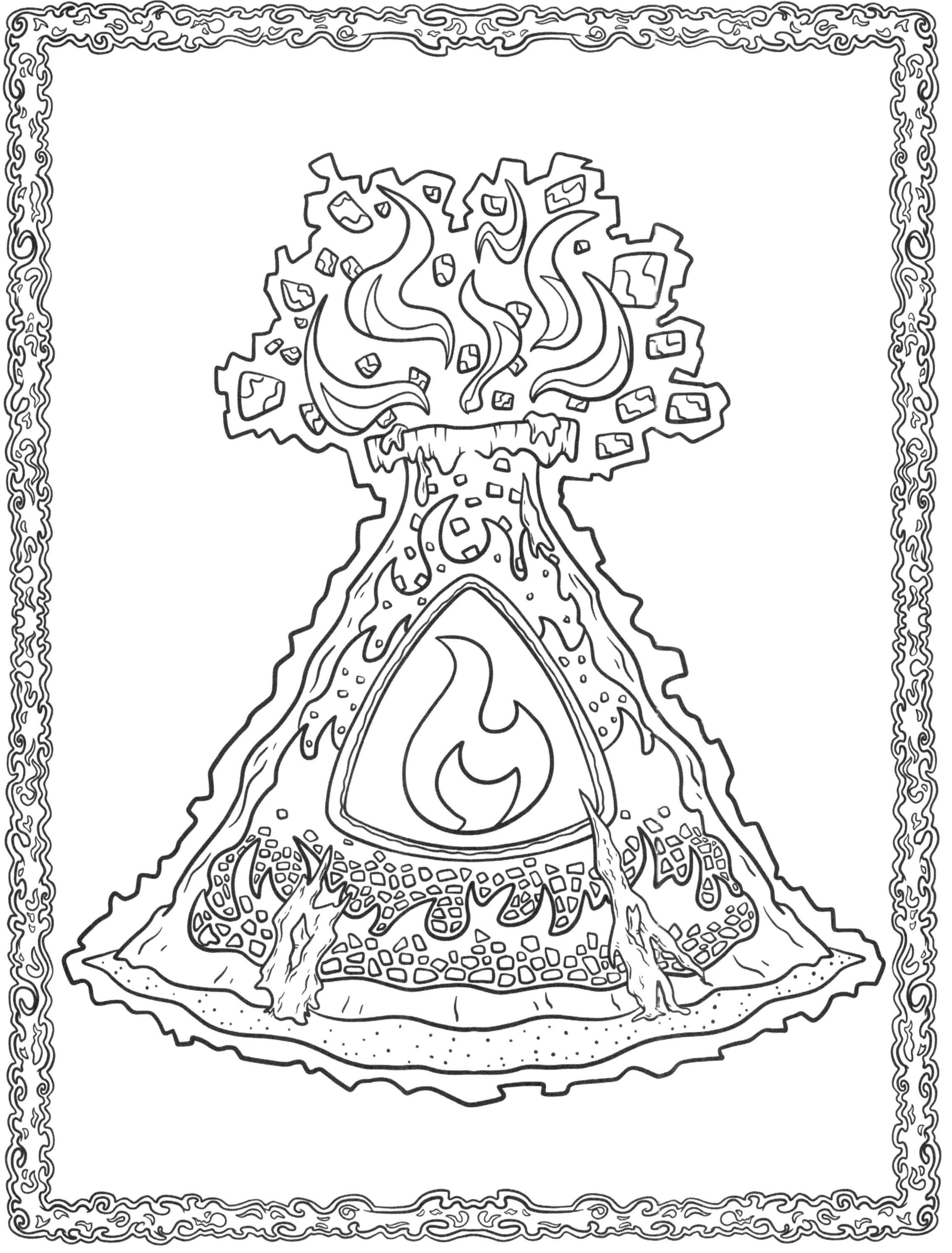

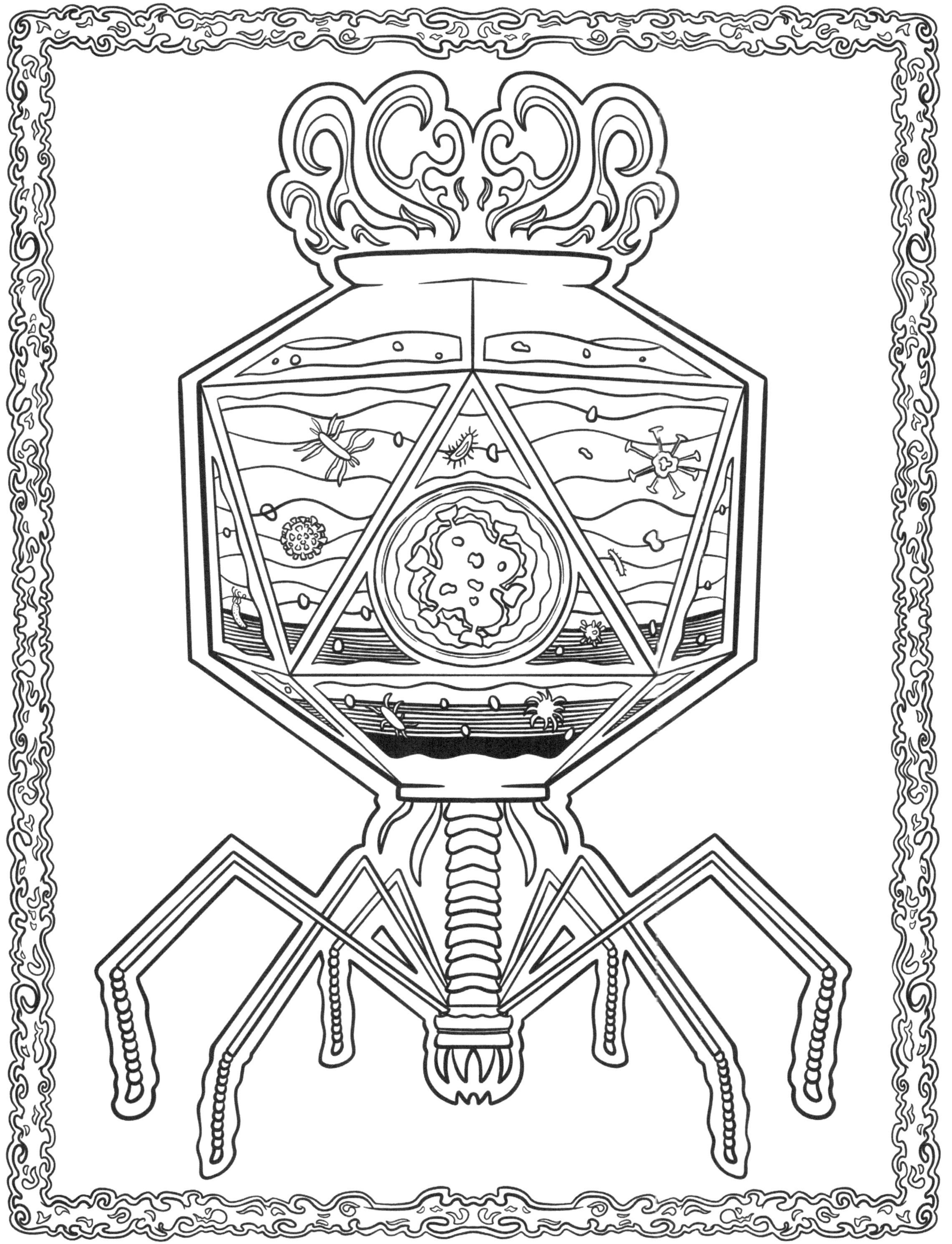

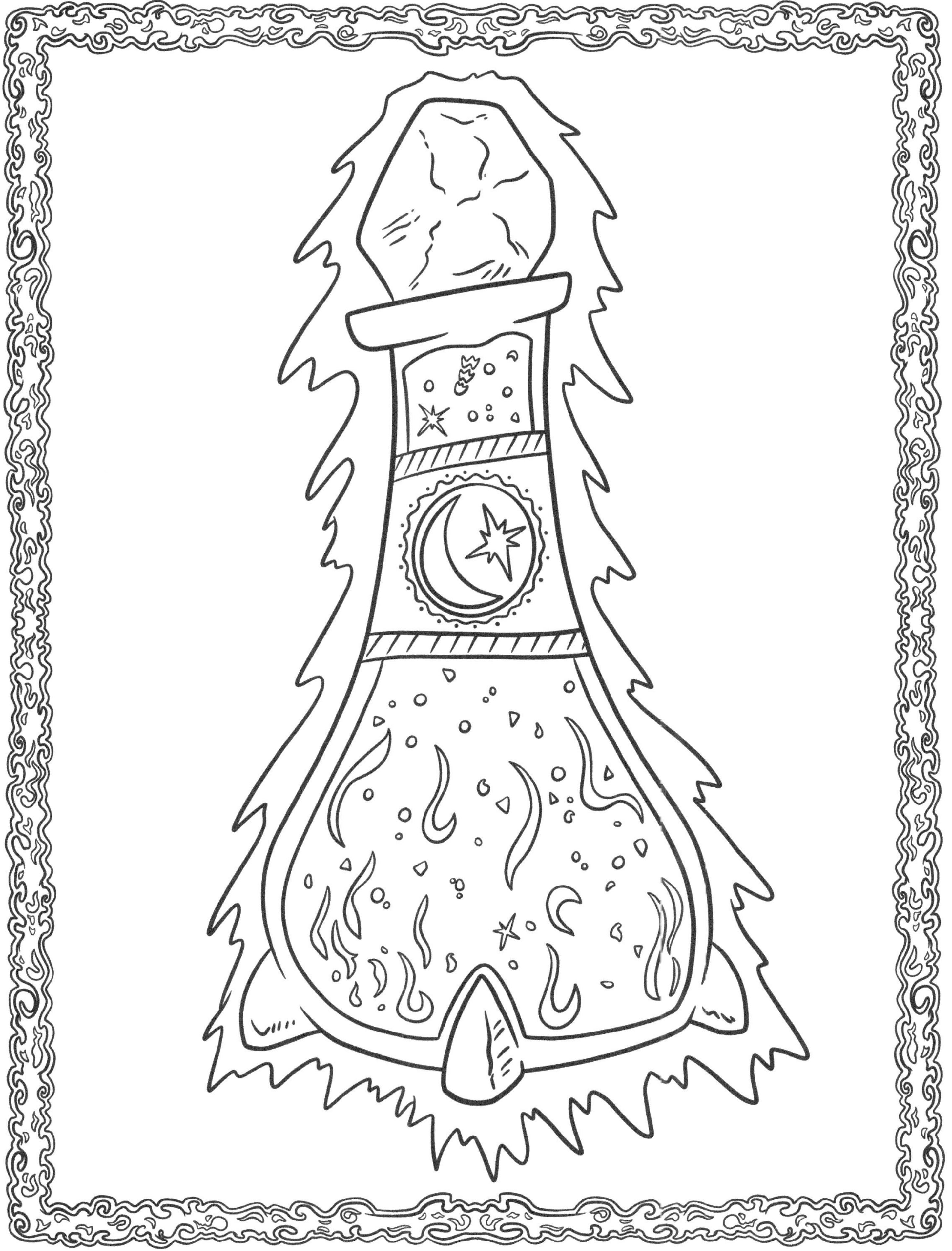

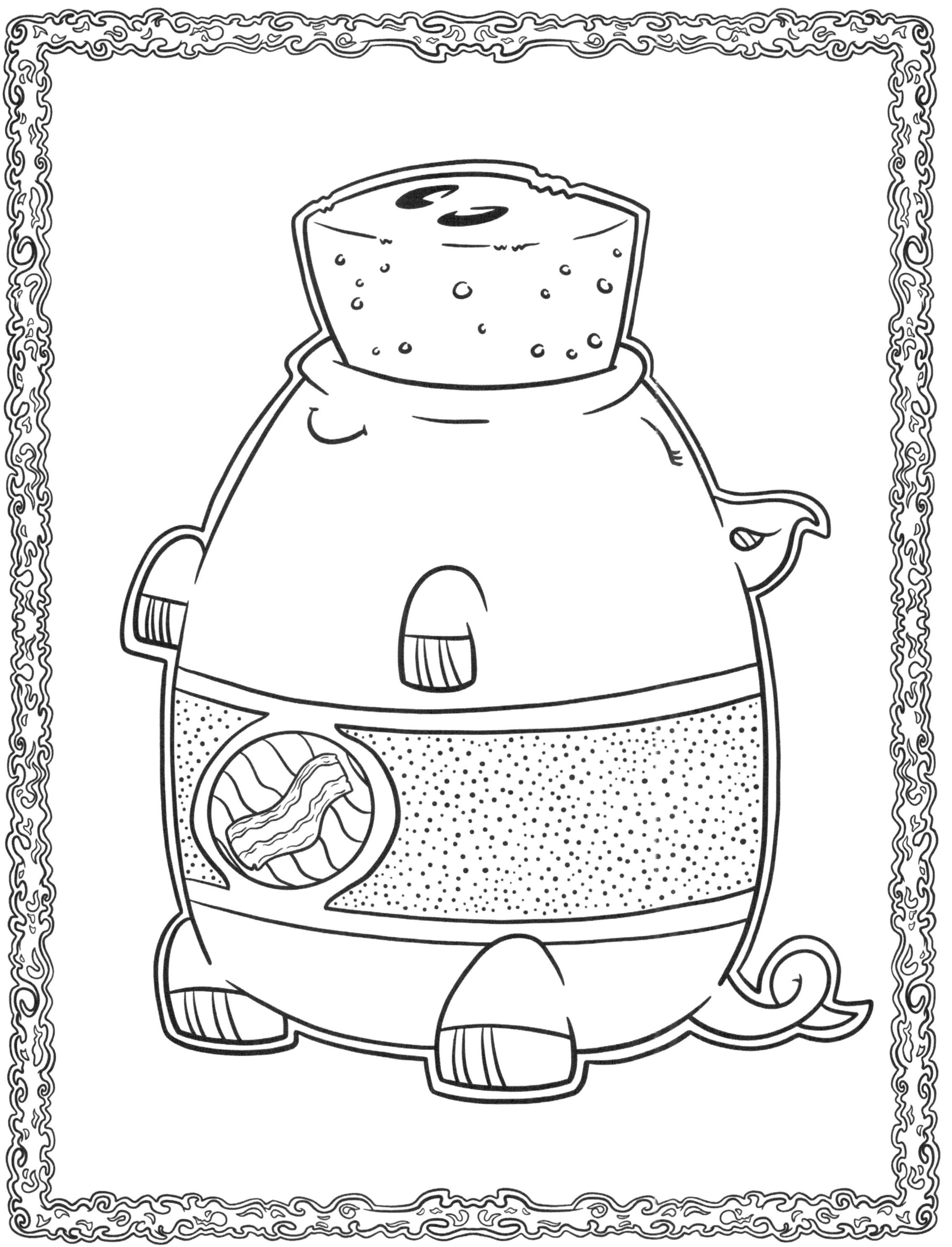

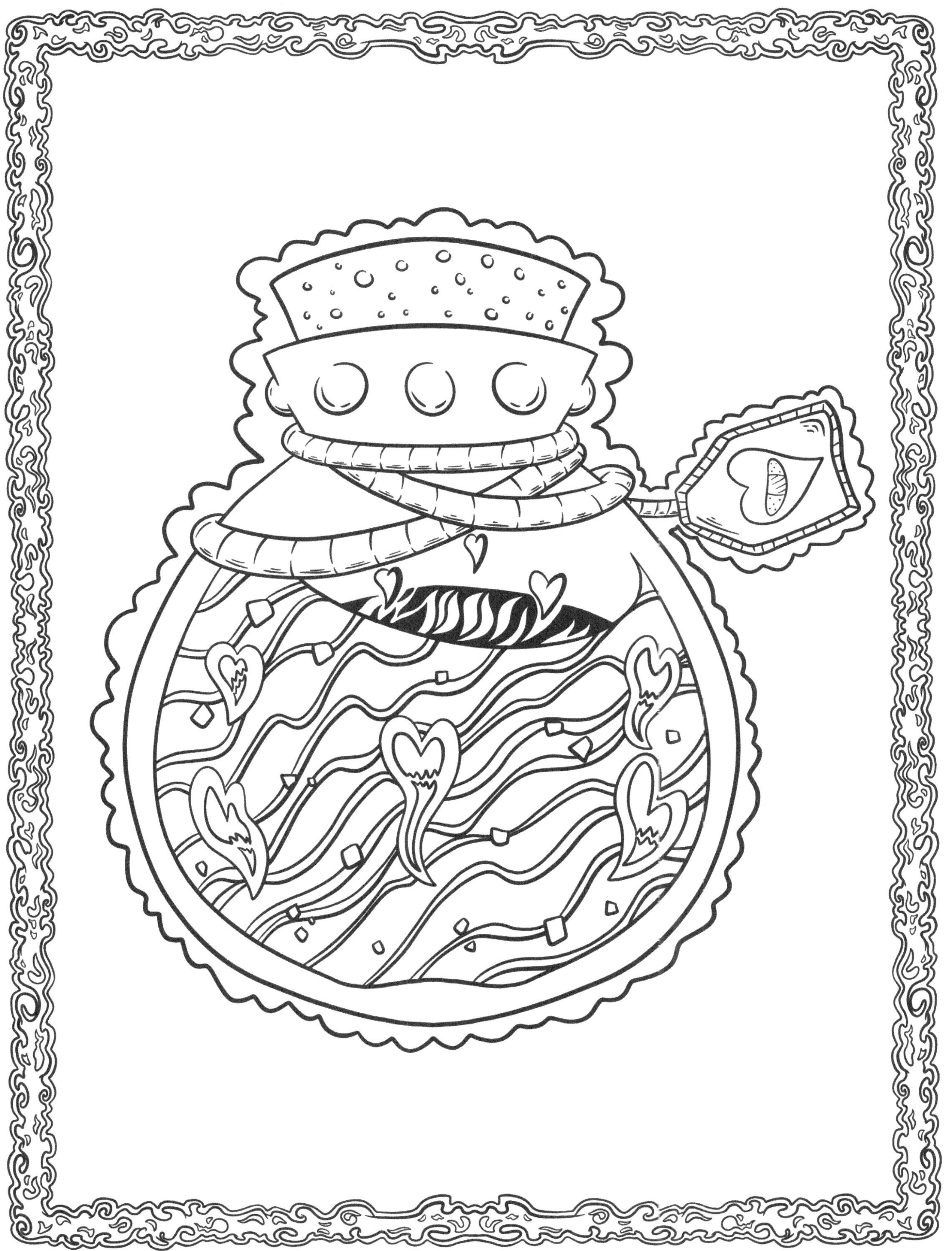

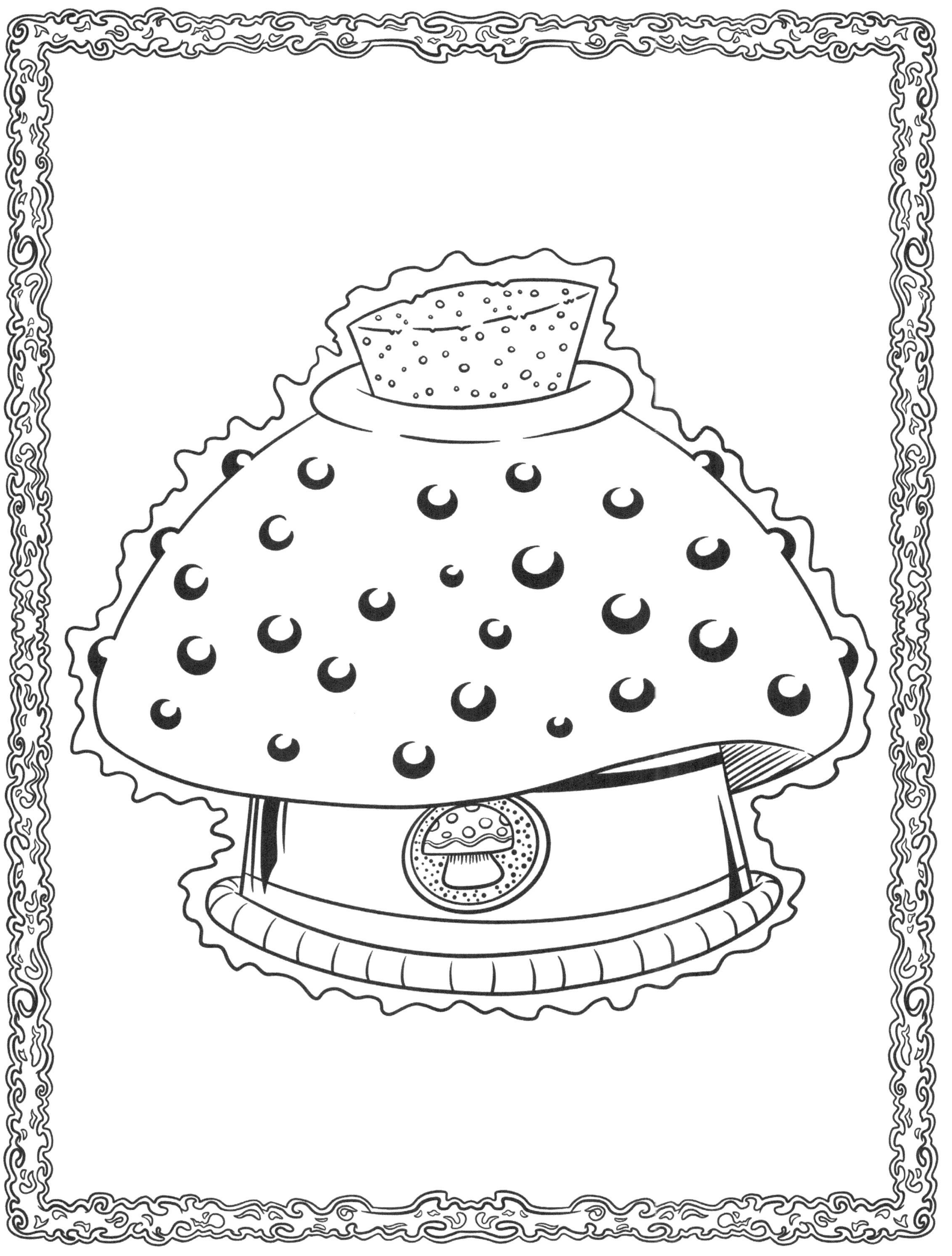

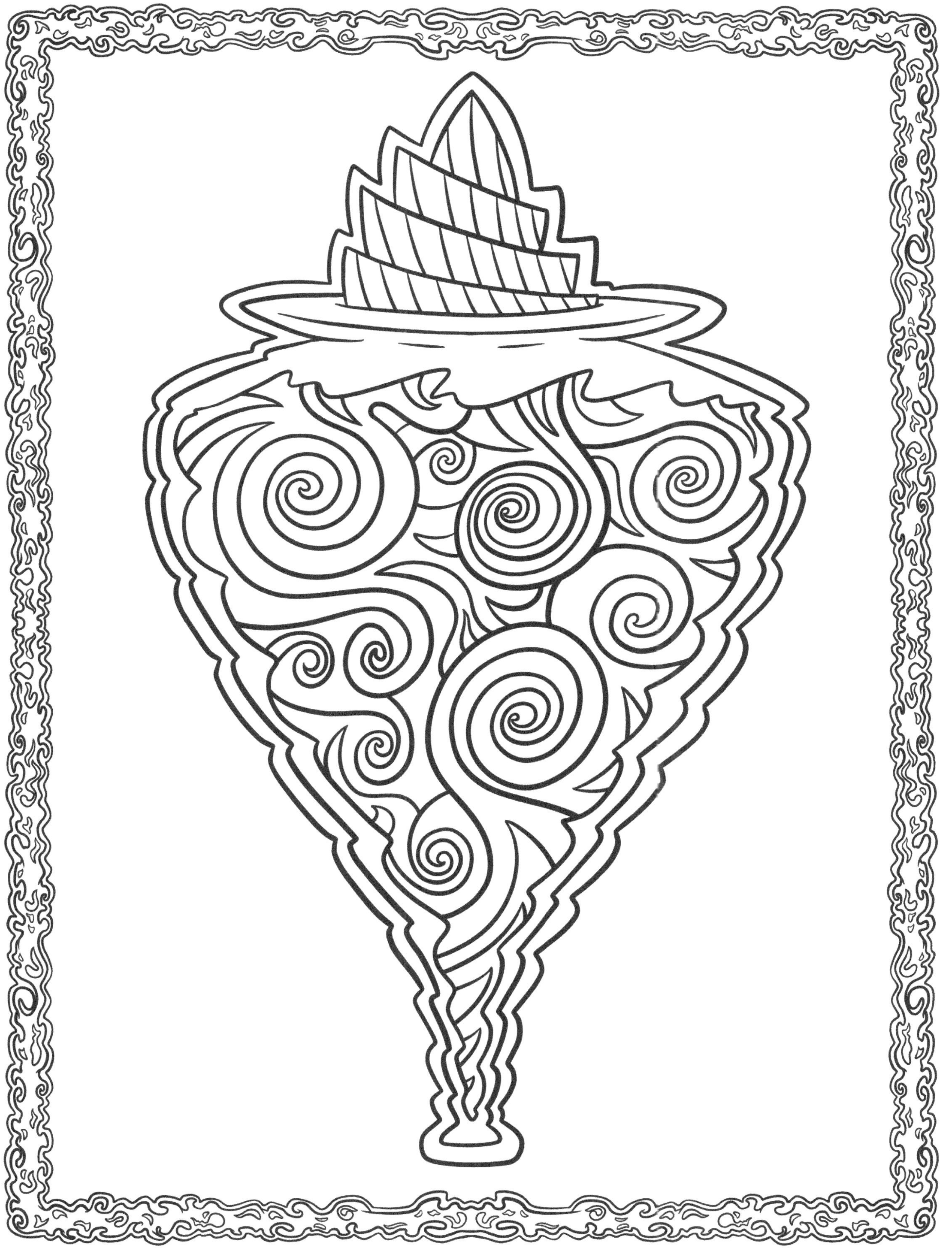

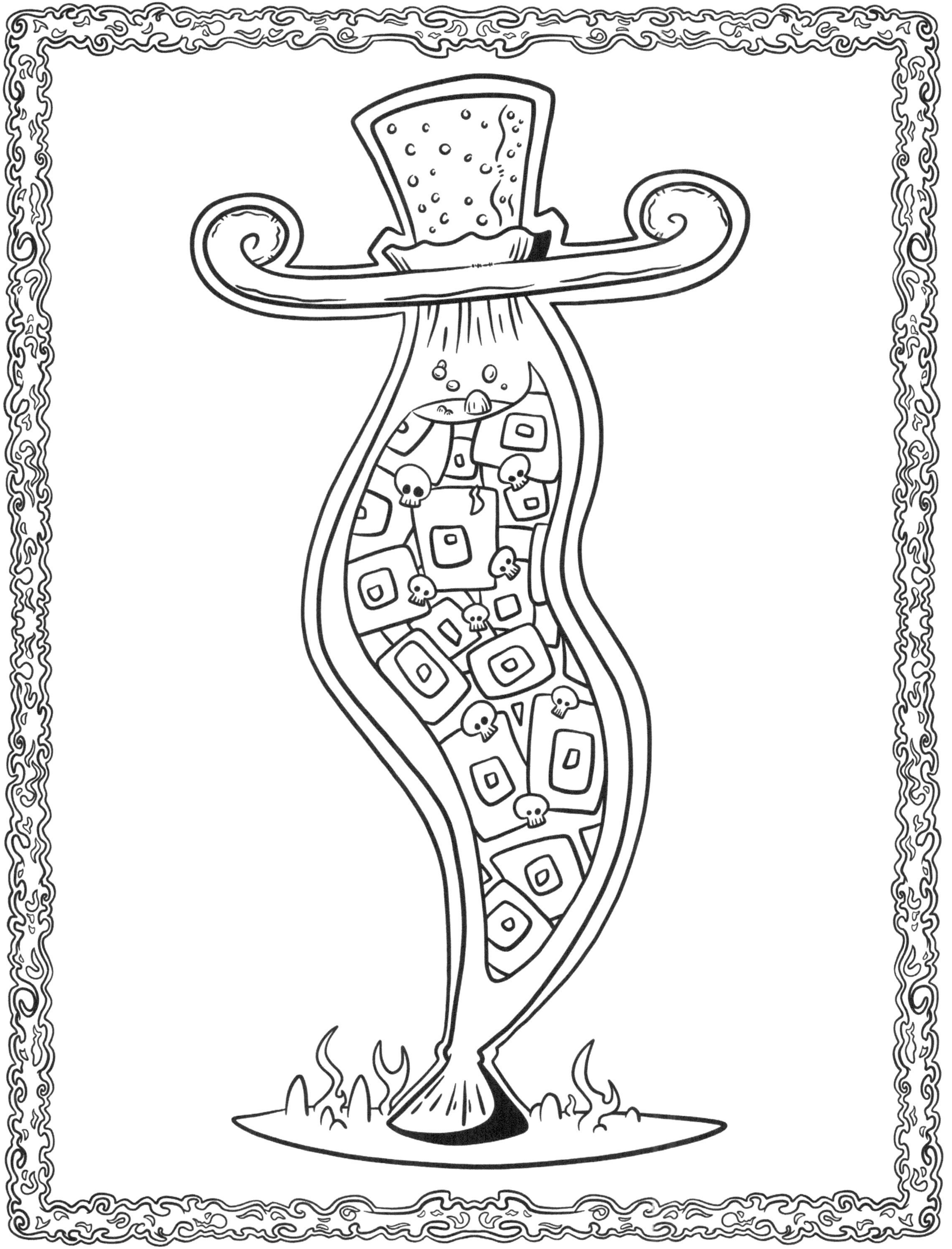

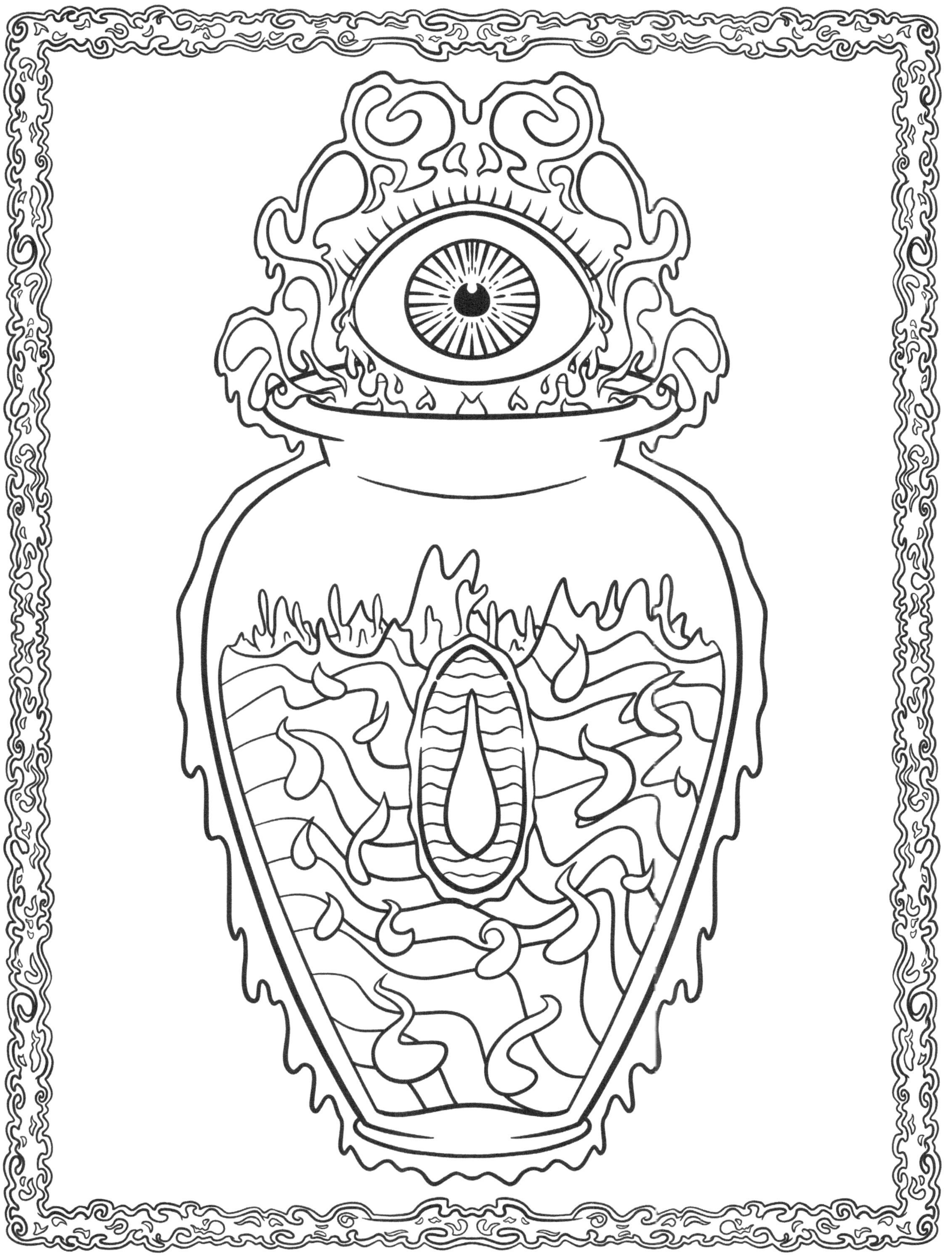

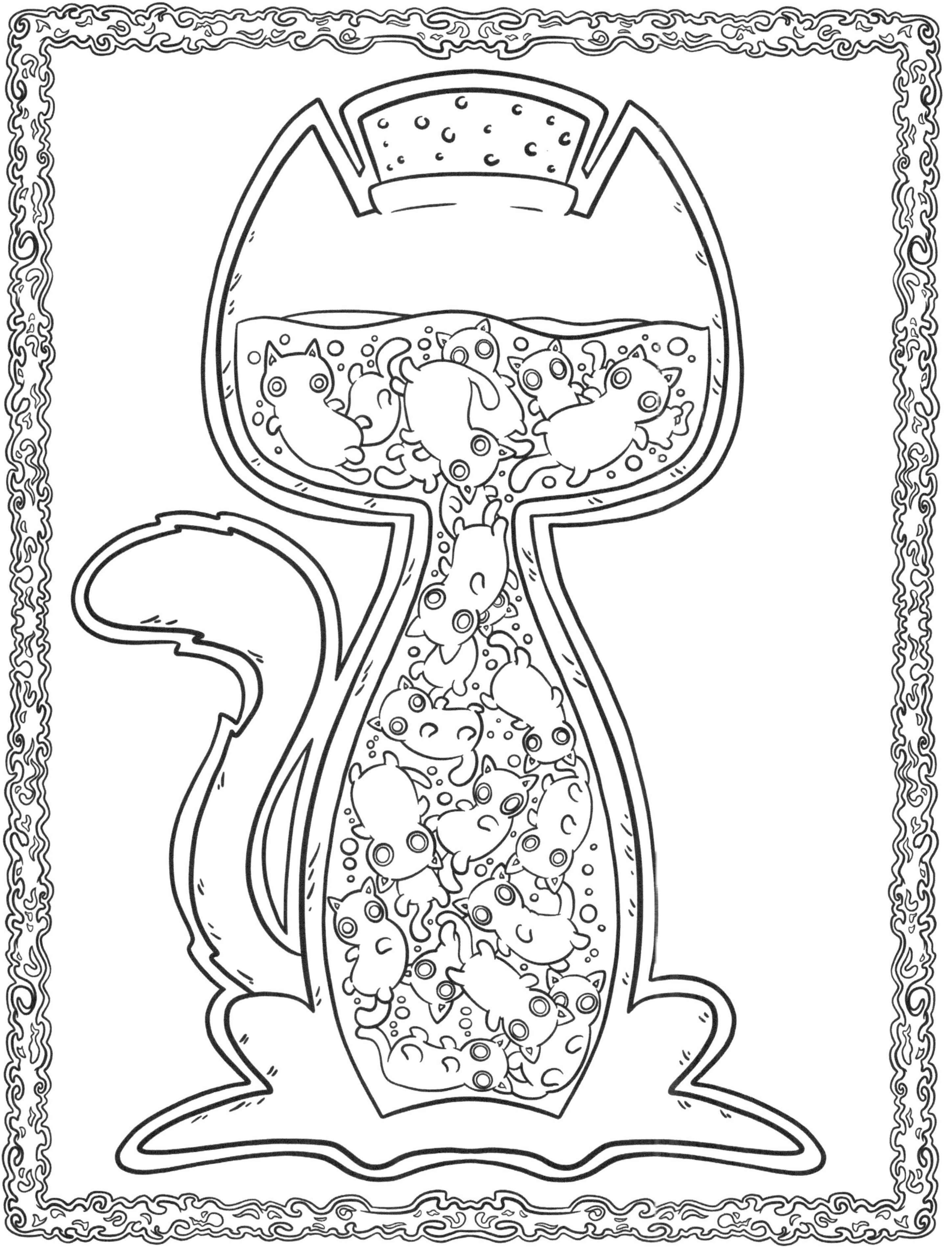

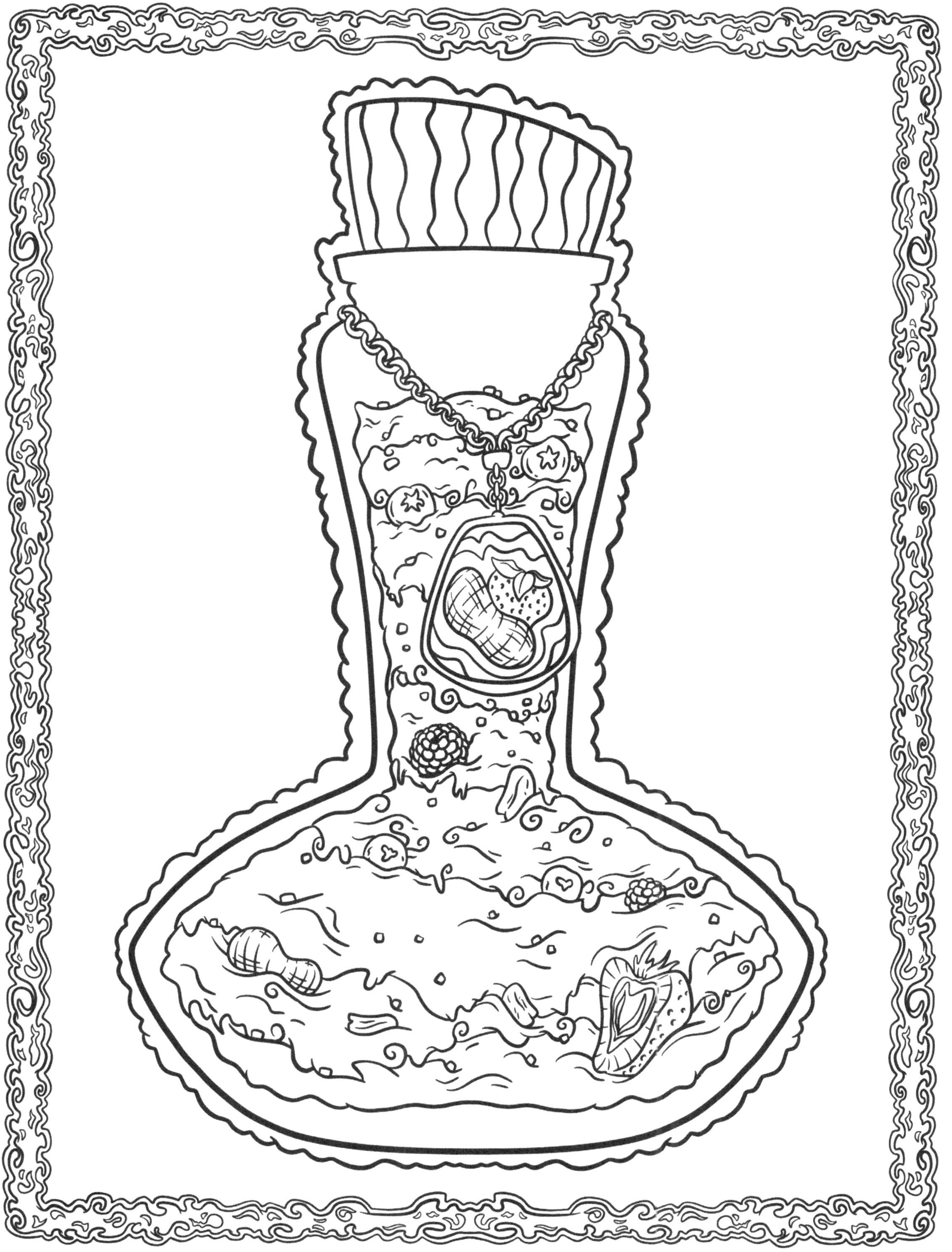

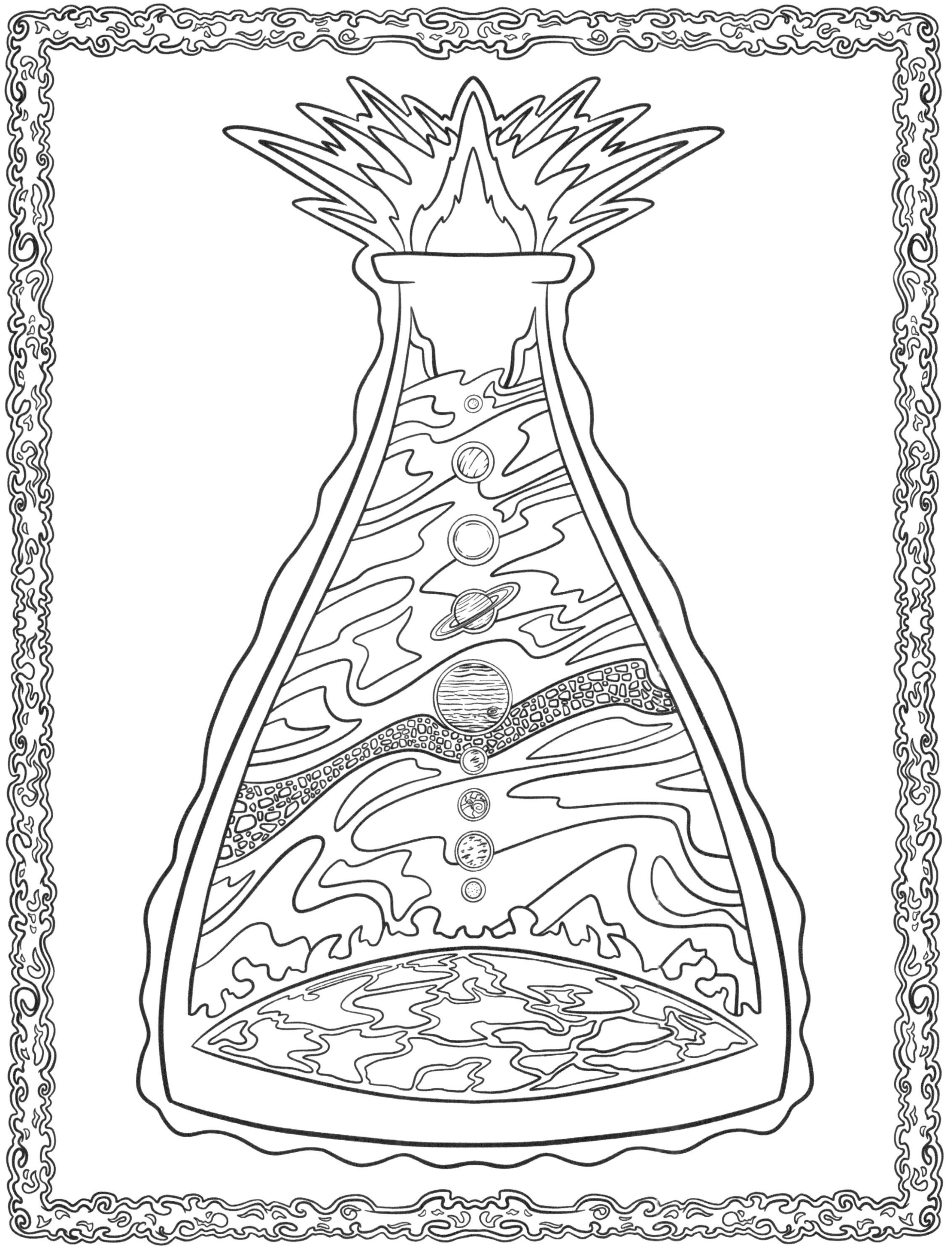

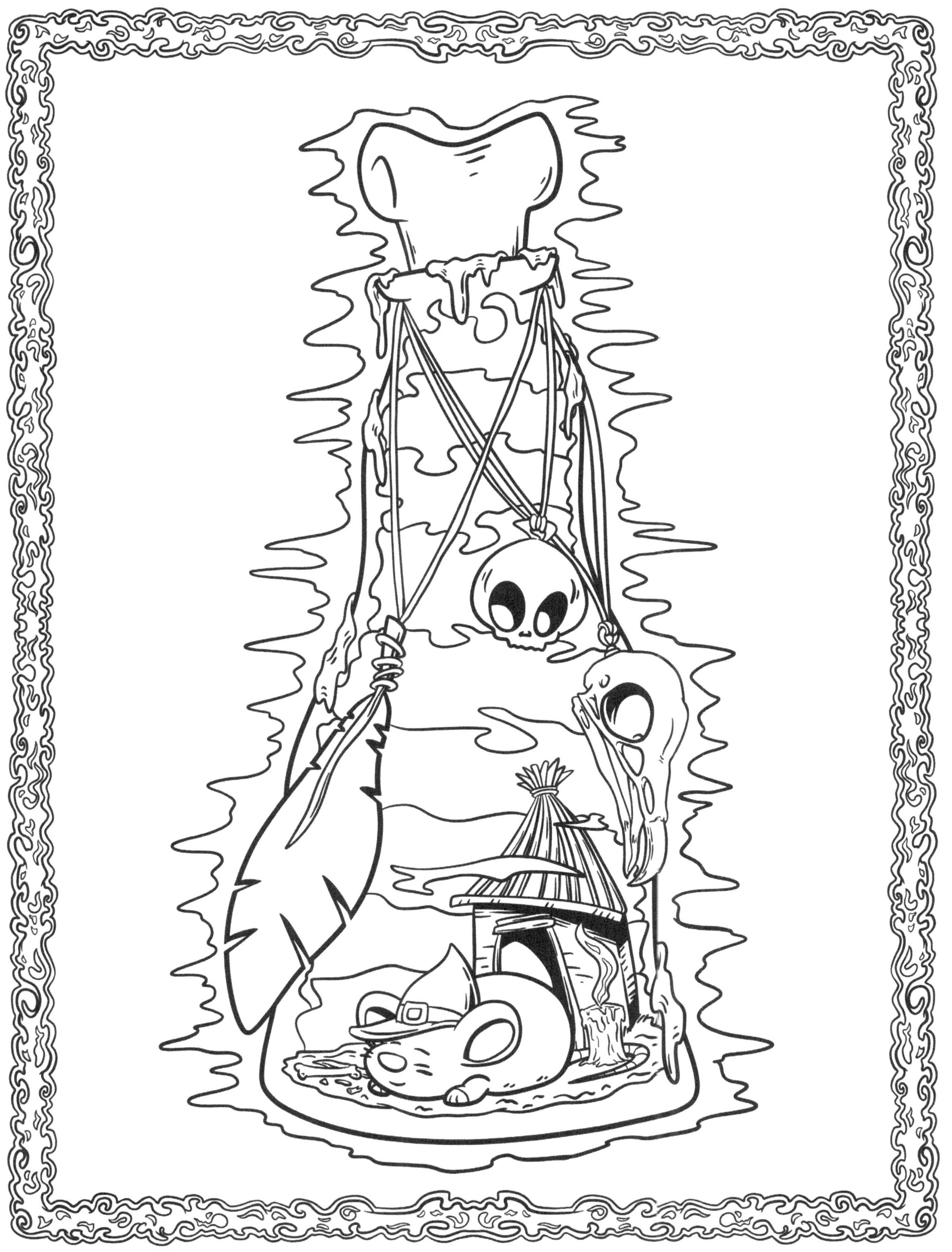

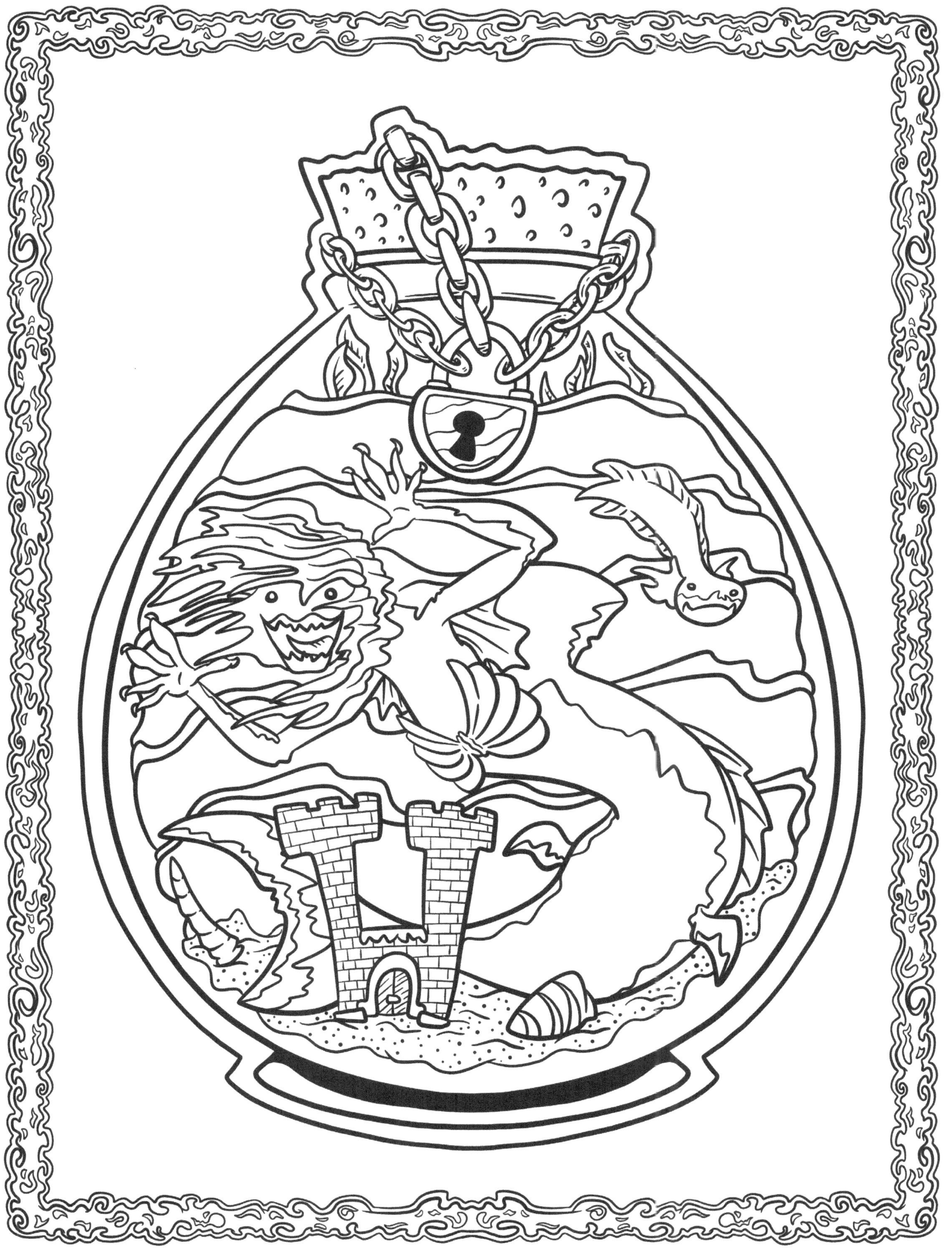

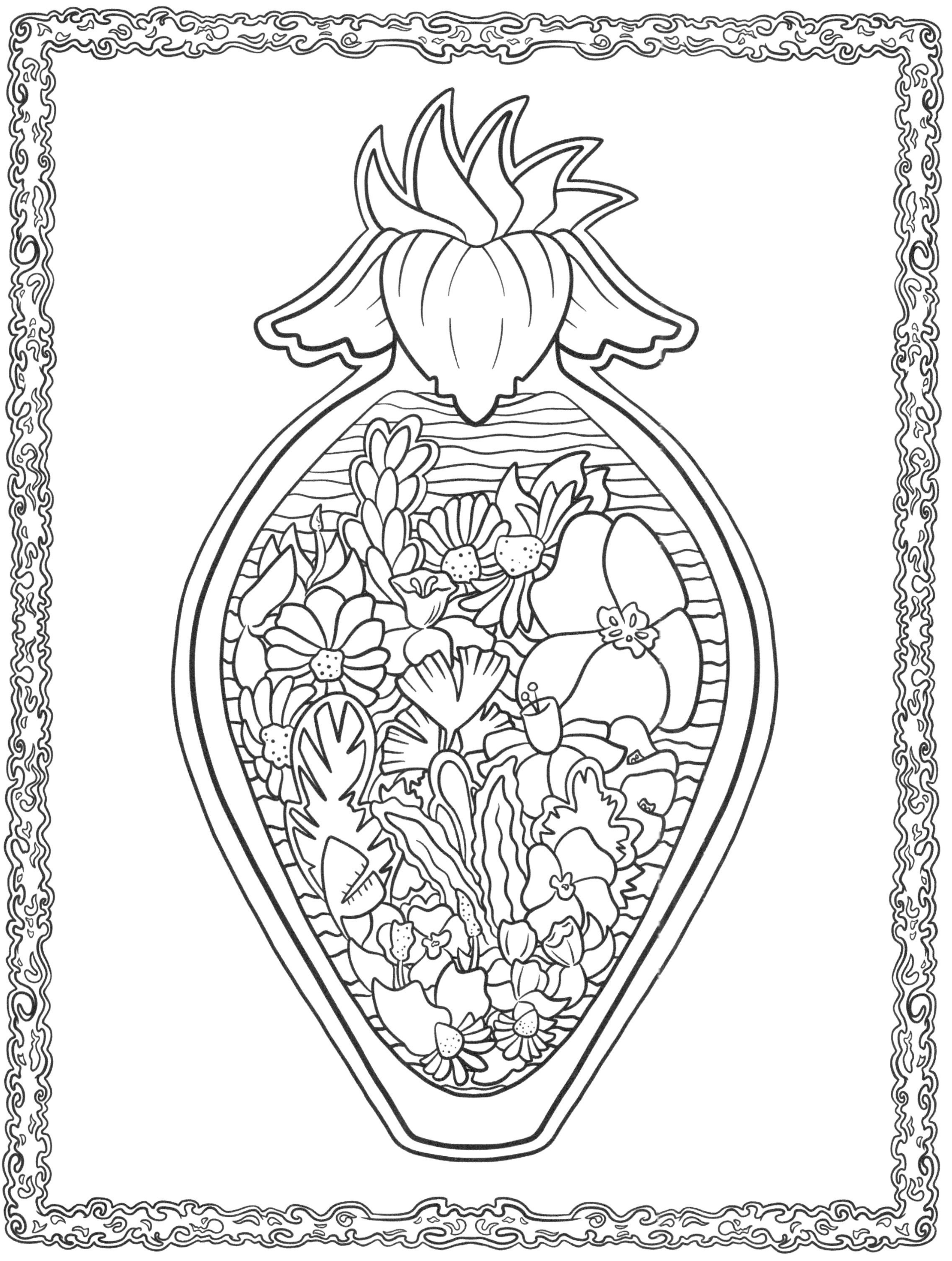

VISIT STUDIO MOONFALL
ZAP IT!
PEW PEW!
VR
THROUGH THE MAGIC OF SCIENCE!
WWW.MOONFALL360.COM

FIND YOUR NEXT BOOK AT STUDIO MOONFALL

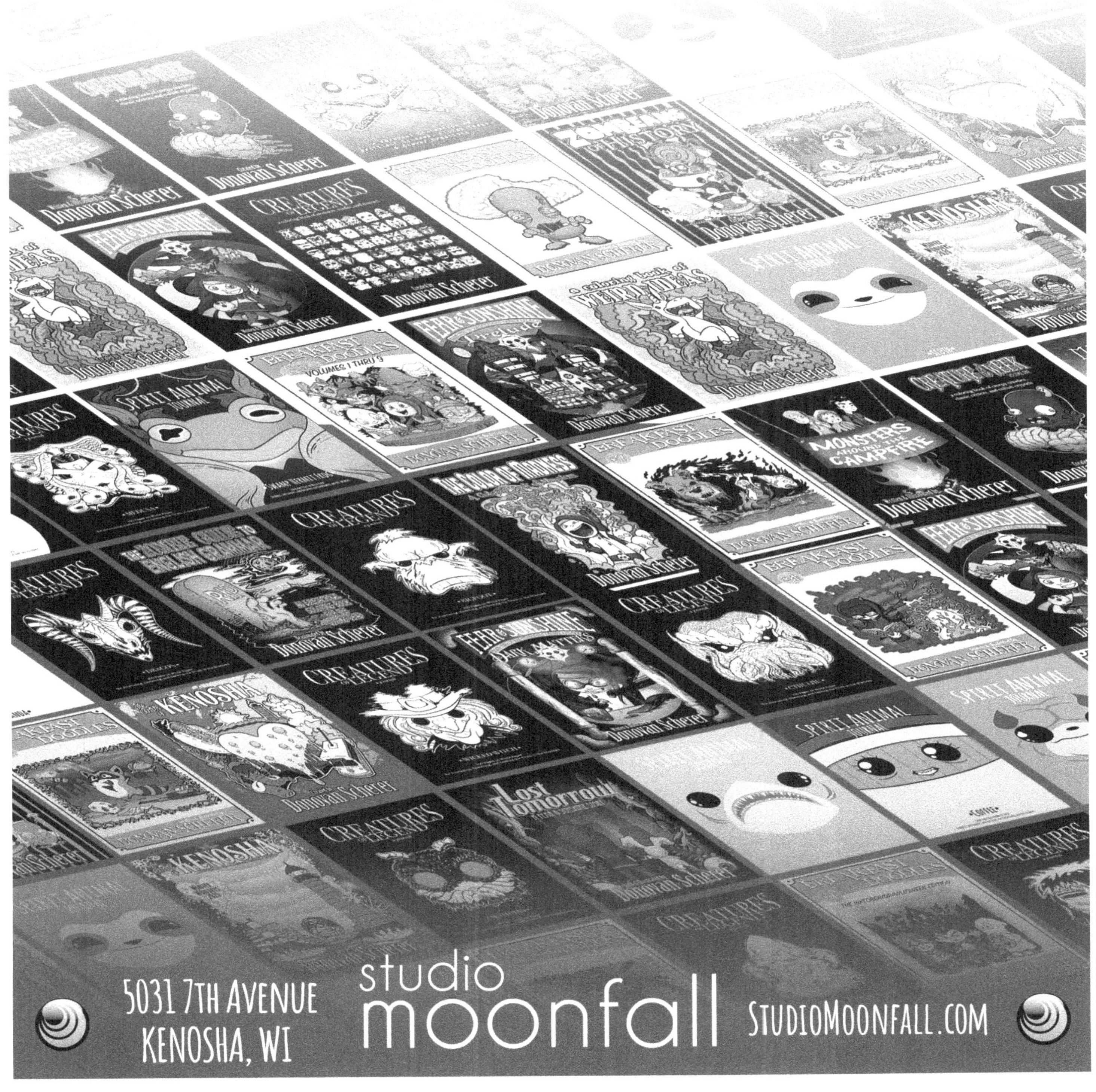